almonds are members of the peach family

almonds are members of the peach family

Sempre in bocca al lupo,
ACA, 2023

stephanie sauer

Noemi
PRESS

Published By Noemi Press, Inc. A Nonprofit Literary Organization.
www.noemipress.org

Cover and Book Design by Steve Halle

ISBN: 978-1-934819-85-2

this book is dedicated to

Billiemae Alice
1932-2018

Doodle & Sweet P

and to all the ancestors,
past and future.

contents

patchwork

... permaneceu inédita, até que eu,
cuja mãe e avós morreram cedo,
de parto, sem discusar
a transmitisse a meus futuros,
enormemente admirada
de uma dor tão alta,
de uma dor tão funda,
de uma dor tão bela,
entre tomates verdes e carvão,
bolor de queijo e cólica.
　　　　　　　—Adélia Prado, "Linhagem"

"Trying to find through these very material means, answers to particular questions. History has to get onto the floor as a material presence."
　　　　　　　—William Kentridge, *Six Drawing Lessons*

Someday I will learn this language.

Rio, the city, has many mouths. Each one houses gums hot from infection reaching into arteries. Rio, the city, does not resist personification. Rio, the city, will eat you. It will suck you and serenade you and swallow the crackle of your bones whole. Rio, the city, has no regard for survival, only for living at the epidural edge—at the moment blood pushes pores open, releases scent. The air is composed of saline and the once living. At certain circumferences, their weight calcifies into matter. I bump into one on the way to buy groceries and it slices my arm. I hold the cut with my opposing hand and an incision forms from the inside of my skin, letting air in but no blood out. Rio, the city, becomes home not because it, too, is a postcard like California Gold Country, but because it, too, fails to digest its dead.

Dog begging outside a bar. Coffee on the factory roof in a lawn chair. I try to read there in the sun a spell. I eat a package of Biscoito Globo leftover from the event we hosted this past weekend. I think of the Candelária I passed early this morning on the bus, consider what happened there: eight homeless children rounded up and shot by police, left for dead on a night in 1993. I wrap books for online purchase orders. I worry. I unpack my studio. I teach myself again how to appliqué. I read. I shoo pigeons from the rooftop. I talk to a theatre-maker about a theatre she is making while on my way to pee. I think about the photograph of my mother's tumor-infected uterus that is now removed from her body. At lunch I run into the contractor and the porter in the place I can buy a plate of chicken, okra, and beans for two dollars if I don't add rice. I walk to the post office at the bus depot; the other was just shut down after its workers were held up twice with machine guns. I call my partner to confirm a zip code. I do not carry a smart phone. I wonder what will come of us. I want to keep sewing things, appliquéing things until life is whole again.

SUCOS & SANDUÍCHES

obvious in that unseen way
of how now I have — or am in
danger — of having everything
usurped by her life. Her

[AUGUST 2012, RIO DE JANEIRO]

I take the 170 bus to my studio, pass in front of the National Archive.
New banners announce that the archives from the dictatorship are
now open to the public.

-

[SEPTEMBER 2012, RIO DE JANEIRO]

All this textile, costura, embroidery in the streets and fairs and gal-
leries homes me.

Making takes form, devours form. I am drawn to new mediums. I
take up stitching. Again. I collect fabrics, threads, twenty-five cent

quilting manuals from the thrift store down the hill. I gather. I take sudden notice of tapestries and handmade patterns. I consider domesticity, craft, and economies changing. I link these to histories of bodies. I think of shifts brought about by activism. I practice. I sew gifts for friends. I thread the machine from memory, forget how to thread a bobbin. Remembering takes half an hour. I sew pieces into patterns for pleasure and to remember. Longing dampens the room, causes dew. I sit down and I write. I write through. I write between stitches. I have to reshape outworn narratives, write into myself new stories. Only then can the making continue.

Patchwork onto muslin backing, whip stitch down. Attach back fabric at 2.5" larger (1.5"/side); turn edges in and self-bind. Trim filling to 0.25" smaller on all sides.

- - - - - - - - - - - - - - - -

1992, NEVADA COUNTY, CALIFORNIA: She takes the child's beating heart in her warm hands and holds it until it softens, until it knows it is safe to open. She sings stories so it will remember things it has never felt. She lulls its redness with her touch. When the heart opens, she pours in all her love and all her fears with it. She pours in all her dreaming and her bruises. She touches its tissues to her swollen lips and weeps. The muscle grows bigger with her tears. The muscle grows tender, skittish to the touch. She sets a kettle on the stove and stirs in possibility, measuring out worries in her palm before sprinkling them in. She ladles the brine into a bowl and serves it with oyster crackers. She spreads the heart with a butter knife on toast and tells the child to eat, to help herself to more.

they sent word back to relatives." Like all good hillsmen, Jimmy has a lively sense of the past, for the hills speak powerfully of continuity. He recalls nostalgically

-

1982–PRESENT, NEVADA COUNTY, CALIFORNIA: Grandma tells me about her two chipped teeth and 137 bruises, four children, three miscarriages, lost the second after being socked in the stomach, surgery, chronic blood clots, watching her eldest child beaten—once, doors nailed shut, losing the promotion, sugar in the gas tank, rape.

Grandpa tells me about how he *had nothin'*. How, when he got back from the war, the Navy dropped him off in Nevada City, and he had to walk all the way to the ranch because there was no phone then— twenty miles of river grade. How when he got there, his own dog didn't even recognize him. How this broke him in places wartime didn't touch.

-

2010, PLACER COUNTY, CALIFORNIA: A friend asks: "Where is my purple heart? My father got one in Vietnam, but what about the rest of us who still have to fight the war he brought back home?"

2003, NEVADA COUNTY, CALIFORNIA: *I know I'm going to die, I just wish I'd get it over with sooner,* he told his mother. Or at least that's what Grandma told me. His body had been withering ever since he was three. Ever since we played marbles and he let me win at Clue, Monopoly. The nerves, they said, had no more padding. Thirty years without a doctor's visit, driving a nine-shift, logging below the summit. Fifty years since the stroke at three. They had said it was encephalitis to cover up the beatings he witnessed. Just huddled his little boy body into a corner and screamed. Fifty years and now he slips, bleeds from the skull all over the carpets. When I am not there. When my aunt is out of town. When he doesn't listen to the recommendations, wants it to end. He frightens me. A body without the command of a human, its uncertainty, the possibility of spasm, buckled joints that stall out at the intersection. Or worse, at that freeway crossing near Bloomfield. But he made it—thirty years of hauling log to sit on a couch by a wood-burning stove in a stick-frame home and wait to die.

-

[2014, NEVADA COUNTY, CALIFORNIA]

The Veterans Affairs Hospital postpones treatment for Grandpa's cancer complications caused from exposure to the atomic bomb testing at Bikini Atoll while he served in the US Navy. His contemporaries are dying off as the VA cancels appointments, puts off treatments, testing. What happens when we don't look too closely at these effects of war, at our own histories? At what they do to a body, to a life, to the bodies and lives of our babies?

2014, NEVADA COUNTY, CALIFORNIA: My nephew is born 12:55 on a Sunday to a local sheriff who tells me that the most common calls in our hometown are to report domestic abuse and suicide.

In an article entitled "Trait vs. Fate" in the May, 2013 issue of Discovery, Dan Hurley discusses the epigenetic programming research of Moske Szyf and Michael Meaney, saying:

> According to the new insights of behavioral epigenetics, traumatic experiences in our past, or in our recent ancestors' past, leave molecular scars adhering to our DNA. . . . Our experiences, and those of our forebears, are never gone, even if they have been forgotten. They become a part of us, a molecular residue holding

fast to our genetic scaffolding. The DNA remains the same, but psychological and behavioral tendencies are inherited. You might have inherited not just your grandmother's knobby knees, but also her predisposition toward depression caused by the neglect she suffered as a newborn. . . . Like grandmother's vintage dress, you could wear it or have it altered. The genome has long been known as the blueprint for life, but the epigenome is life's Etch A Sketch: shake it hard enough, and you can wipe clean the family curse.

–

[MAY 2013, RIO DE JANEIRO]

The sound of the machine comforts—the repetition of the pressure foot beating cotton, the slow but known expanding of patterns in my hands. A stagnation. This need to clear the heart. Clear the arteries. Break open the decay covering the real.

Embroidery has always been a deservedly popular hobby. It stimulates the imagination and at the same time provides an island of calm in the midst of a hurly-burly world.

My friends and I joked in high school that the street on which our grandparents lived should be renamed Wife Beater Lane, and not for the cotton apparel. It was the first suburb in town, and nearly every post-war home hid a violent story that had been stricken from the Greatest Generation documentaries airing on TV. We all knew the stories: cops who responded to calls by driving the men around until they sobered up, then dropping them back off at home. No consequences. No shame. Now that same street, like so many suburban streets in this country, is home to meth labs and hydroponic pot farms. The police are called out for a different kind of danger, a danger seen as real.

–

My grandpa is a legend, I hear at the local diner, taking unnecessary risks with his life and his scrappy equipment to haul log in the Sierras and keep his business afloat.

My grandpa is a legend, I hear.

–

2013: A United Nations Office on Drugs and Crimes "Global Study on Homicide" finds that of all women killed in 2012, nearly half were killed by intimate partners or family members.

2013: A World Health Organization study published under the title, "Global and Regional Estimates of Violence against Women" found that an average of one in three women around the world "have experienced either physical and/or sexual intimate partner violence or non-partner sexual violence." Other studies reveal that only fourteen percent of women report their experiences of intimate partner violence.

Emergency Shelters - Chicago

Greenhouse Shelter - 773-278-4110
Apna Ghar - 773-334-4663
Family Rescue - 773-375-8400
House of the Good Shepard - 773-935-3434
Neopolitan Lighthouse - 773-638-0227

[10 ABRIL 2013, RIO DE JANEIRO]
6:45am. Transcribing the words of my grandmother in a backstitch works them out of my skin.

Memories open with the movement of my hands: quilting bees with my mother. 4-H sewing classes. All the practical applications for beautiful handmade things, the creativity and company of other women.

-

[5 MAIO 2013, RIO DE JANEIRO]
Finished embroidering the first kerchief yesterday. Have yet to start the next one. This work difficult, dangerous. I want to give it up at moments, but can already notice myself becoming scientific about the words of my grandmother. I can talk about them, expose them, detach them from my own voice for a change.

I have not left the house in days.

The backside of my stitching is not neat and tidy like examples I've seen, like my mother's. I am not worried about being messy, following patterns. This, freeing.

X X X X X X X X X XX X X X X X X X X X

finally I took a test
and passed so high
I couldn't believe it
cause he kept telling
how stupid I was how
stupid I was and every-
thing and I went to work
and was made supervisor in
a year I would've been second
high but he went and
busted my door in poured
said he's
gonna
pour

sugar in my
gas tank

— — — — — —

— — — — — —

— — — — — —

— — — — — —

— — — — — —

— — — — — —

batting

"People who have survived atrocities . . . witnesses as well as
victims are subject to the dialectic of trauma. It is difficult for an
observer to remain clearheaded and calm, to see more than a few
fragments of the picture at one time, to retain all the pieces and to
fit them together. It is even more difficult to find a language that
conveys fully and persuasively what one has seen."
—Judith Herman, M.D., *Trauma and Recovery*

I give my head to clear thinking
My heart to greater loyalty
My hands to larger service
For my club, my community, my country, and my world.
—4-H Pledge

The inner lining
of the cups of the first bra
I bought myself
with the first paycheck
from my first job
with the college degree
that was the first in my family
are stained
from weeping.

My breasts are weeping.

This is not poetry. Weeping is the medical term for the seepage that occurs from a hereditary eczema enflamed by acute emotional distress, which may or may not also be hereditary.

The weeping does not cause the staining. The broken tissues of my areoles leak a clear fluid. The comfrey root I boil in water and make into a salve is what leaves traces.

[2013, RIO DE JANEIRO]

BROKEN

    BROKEN

is a word I want to stitch across all the seams in this quilt.

I have not sought release forms to record or publish my grand-mother's stories. They resist the restrictions of copyright law. Her story is part of my story, but it is not my story. The tearing away requires vigilance, a seam ripper, and stumbling.

"Just imagine what she could have done if she had had a little sup-port," an uncle laments. He swears I have inherited her fight. I have seen what a woman's life can become when she gives up her grip on something essential. She turns brittle, evaporates, and is replaced by a viciousness no human can temper, least of all herself. I have seen this. I come from a place where such brittle lives become ash and scatter, contaminate the ground water. Poisons us all. I find it hard to live without battling. I have no idea, really, what a life without fight would look like, and sometimes I think I keep the demons close because fighting them is all I know.

Slowly, slowly, I let go and make up the life I want to be living. I in-vent. This is another kind of fight, this battling off the world outside to keep myself whole, to keep the making alive. But at least it is a different fight. Sometimes.

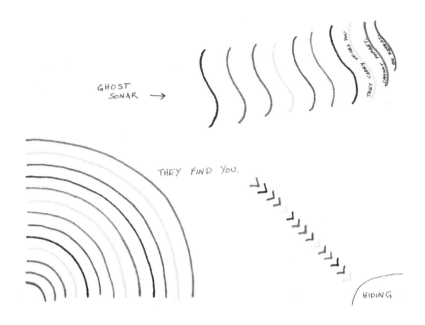

GHOST SONAR →

THEY FIND YOU.

HIDING

[18 SETEMBRO 2012, RIO DE JANEIRO]

Overrun by phantom sightings. I look out into this city and see only what has happened here, though I do not know all the details. The old centro breathes in, expels memories that go undocumented in the books on Rio's splendor for sale in the stalls lining the mouth of the metro. Tourist guides note history in framed boxes set off to the side of the main text. This history is meant to add exoticism, humor, intrigue. It adds value in the marketplace. I live in a postcard of carnival, beaches, bunda. I was born in a postcard of the Wild, Wild West. I sensed its holocaust before I ever heard the story. I have collected postcards of other places only to compare them to the sound of their stonework. The romance of newness wears itself threadbare and leaves only holes for the past to rush in. Once we see the horror of a becoming, can we ever see anything else? This has nothing to do with will or deciding to see the good. Places leech their memories whether or not we wish to listen.

2012, RIO DE JANEIRO: I cross the street to the pharmacy. The military police are outside wielding assault rifles, occupying the entrance to the favela down a side street. Rio has just secured their bid for the 2016 Olympics, and there is talk of hiring ex-NYC Mayor Rudy Giuliani to oversee the "clean up" of the city. I notice my visceral response to assault rifles on men in uniform is different from other passers by. I notice myself as foreign in this instance: my response is rage, terror. Milling around me are faces that convey *we are used to this. This is normal.* I mask my reaction. I enter the pharmacy, buy toilet paper, toothpaste. Commerce drones on down the boulevard: *un suco de abacaxi e um pão de queijo, por favor.*

2013, RIO DE JANEIRO: Apathy in a year's time has turned to outrage, action, political mobilization. Protests one million strong all across the country are finding solidarity in a global network of anonymous sites, authors. There is deep fear in the daily proof that life here is not valued. But there has been enough. *Basta já!* There are reverberations of Brazil's past revolutions, of the Arab Spring, of Occupy. There is no face, only moving.

2013, SÃO PAULO: We set up our table at Feira Plana, the largest artist publication fair in the country. Makers are enflamed. The medium itself again becomes an active one, full of nuance and risk. R staffs our table while I float from press to press examining new work, swapping samples, and talking shop. I return to staff our table while she tours the fair. We have become part of a traveling band of independent publishers in a place where independent publishing was long illegal. The fifth largest nation in the world, Brazil was the last in the Americas to acquire a printing press and the last to legalize domestic publishing. By the late 1800s, letterpress and woodblock printers working in the Northeast developed their own Cordel literary tradition with roots in local oral cultures, as well as chapbook and troubadour traditions imported from Europe and Africa by way of the Silk Road. But until the last century, very little commercial printing existed in this country with a landmass ninety-two times that of its colonizer. This legacy is part of the reason Rachel and I have found it difficult to buy paper or print books inside the country: there is no strong tradition of papermaking or commercial printing, and, by extension, a limited number of well-trained printers. We've published thirty-six books—new works by Brazilian authors and artists, translations of Brazilian books into English, and Portuguese translations of books that would not otherwise find space in the mainstream Brazilian market—yet still find it difficult to produce some of our titles. But Brazil now has a thriving community of independent publishers with which we share this struggle. Today at Casa do Povo (The People's House), we are part of a blend of small presses, fine art presses, self-publishers, poster makers, book artists, artist-instructors, cartoonists, zine makers, and poets. Many print with the aid of salvaged technologies that allow hands to smudge ink: letterpress, silkscreen, risograph, Xerox. The immediacy and resilience of our mediums are especially resonant now. Again.

-

2013: I dream I had a studio in an antique shop set up inside an ancient Gothic cathedral in Brazil. One night I left, then come back after closing to track down and disappear a ghost that haunted the place, that was after my beloved. It threatened my family.

There are no monsters here, only ghosts.

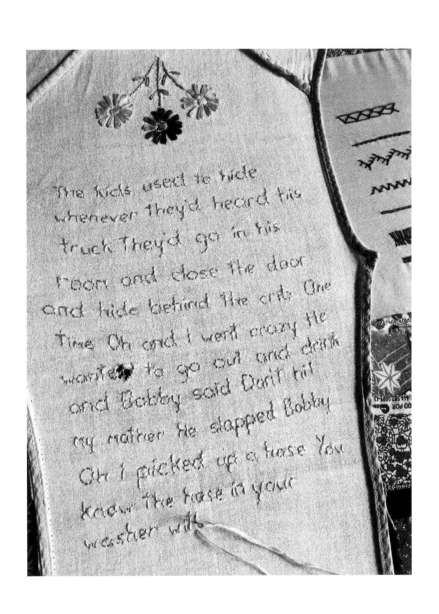

The kids used to hide
whenever they'd heard his
truck They'd go in his
room and close the door
and hide behind the crib One
Time Oh and I went crazy He
wanted to go out and drink
and Bobby said Don't hit
my mother He slapped Bobby
Oh I picked up a hose You
know the hose in your
washer with

[JUNE 2013, RIO DE JANEIRO]

Have had to distance from this stitching. Much. To heal my own flesh outside its heaviness, this hurt. All this bruised little girl flesh. And most of it is not even mine.

-

[AUGUST 2013, RIO DE JANEIRO]

Ironing this old plaid Levi shirt smells of home. Of my trucker uncle. Of Grandma in curlers by the fireside ironing Dad's work clothes after his divorce. Saying *he does so much for us girls*. I cut the shirt at the seams, whittle the fabric into tiny triangles and pin them front-sides-facing to other cottons.

In the studio voices invade, cast doubt. My mother's voice about how my sewing technique is flawed, that I cannot pull off this mess in time for the exhibit. That I do not have the skills to piece together all these unruly fragments. My quilting skills ruptured when our thread broke. I wet the tip, rethread my needle, attempt it anyway.

-

[21 OUTUBRO 2013, RIO DE JANEIRO]

"If we inherit character traits, why not also memories?"

Reading Anaïs Nin's *Diary* all morning. Coffee, eggs, pão, cold feijoada. Up at six, hungover. Amarzem São Thiago last night. Again. A's favorite dive. She left for the ashram early. R still asleep.

Finding Nin's *Diary* to be one of the most brilliant works of literature from the last century, despite her racist exoticizing, gossiping, self-aggrandizement and messiness. But these last three qualities are the very things that make this work brilliant: the project of it, the innovation and courage it took to insist on this writing in diary form at the time of Big Male Writers marking Modernism as territory and vampirizing women, including Nin. In eight years of higher education dedicated to literature and writing, I never studied Nin's work, only dismissed her biography: Henry Miller's lover, author of male-centered erotica.

-

"For every soldier who serves in a war abroad, there are ten children endangered in their own homes. . . . For many people, the war begins at home."
—Bessel Van Der Kolk, MD, *The Body Keeps the Score*

"Trauma's impact comes partly from social factors, such as its influence on how parents interact with their children. But stress also leaves 'epigenetic marks'—chemical changes that affect how DNA is expressed without altering its sequence. A study published this week in Nature Neuroscience finds that stress in early life alters the production of small RNAs, called microRNAs, in the sperm of mice. The mice show depressive behaviors that persist in their progeny, which also show glitches in metabolism."
—Virginia Hughes, "Sperm RNA carries marks of trauma"
(Nature.com: International Weekly Journal of Science, 14 April 2014)

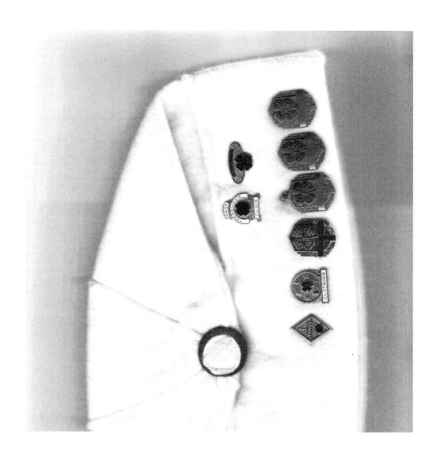

Demonstrations outside in the streets. Policia militar cars, rubber bullets. Lots and lots of rubber bullets. Protesters clapping to the rhythm of *Who Let the Dogs Out?* with protest lyrics.

Getting quotes for mom's boob job. She insists I call it a 'breast augmentation' and says that, with the loss of weight and ovaries from the cancer, they look like two fried eggs hung on nails.

The 4-H schoolhouse down Kentucky Flat Road was a room full of mothers and daughters and the purr of machine needles pounding in and out of cloth.

My baby sister was married on that sewing teacher's farm.

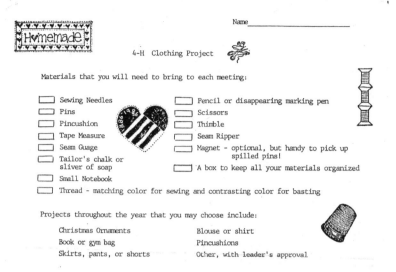

[AUGUST 2013, RIO DE JANEIRO]

Stitching on the machine opens memory: sewing my own clothes after my mother packed up my belongings without notice and left them and me *to save her marriage.* Halter tops, altered jeans, satchels. *The Offspring* playing. I pieced together fabrics then as a way to comfort myself, to call back into my body the moments I loved most with her: making things. Those hours of focus that opened out the universe in unspeakable ways. The wonder of holding up a finished piece, evidence of that other world. It was not just the awe of being able to make anything on our own, but the envelopment in a world that felt more real, more alive than this one. I came back to this world with magic in my palms.

She attempted sutures: gifts stitched by hand, *I love you*s. I stopped trusting the words by the time I turned fourteen.

Now sewing brings the pain back, eases it. It reveals holes in my own loving. I held tight to a divine plan narrative to survive that raw pain, told myself it was an experience I needed, one that pushed me to leave the hills. And while today I doubt this story, I can't help but think I might have been onto something. I loved that rural life. I loved that quiet making, even the practicality of it. I may well have settled early, too, into a life that wasn't quite mine. Maybe the leaving *was* necessary. But living has a way of bending you until you doubt every rigid narrative you've ever held about yourself. So maybe the story I crafted was true. But maybe, too, I have just done the best I could do and this body that stitches shows its pain too plainly.

patch (păch), *n.* [ME. *pacche.*] **1.** Something like the original material used to mend, fill up, or cover a hole, rent, breach, or weak spot. **2.** A small piece of black silk or court plaster stuck on the face, esp. to heighten beauty. **3.** Hence: **a** A small piece; bit; scrap. **b** A passage; excerpt. **c** A spot or blotch differing in color from the ground. **d** A small area or plot distinguished from its surroundings; as, a *patch* of trees. — *v. t.* **1.** To mend, repair, strengthen, etc., with a patch or patches. **2.** To make out of patches, scraps, etc.; hence, to put together hastily or clumsily. **3.** To settle; adjust; as, to *patch* up a quarrel. — **Syn.** See MEND. — **patch'er,** *n.*

patch'work' (păch'wûrk'), *n.* **1.** Something made of incongruous, unrelated scraps or parts; a jumble. **2.** A cover (as for a quilt) or other piece of work made by sewing together pieces of cloth of various sizes, shapes, and colors. Cf. CRAZY QUILT. **3.** A variegated or checkered appearance, design, or scene; as, a *patchwork* of fields.

patch test. *Med.* A test for determining a person's susceptibility

[2013, RIO DE JANEIRO]

I don't know quite how to break it open, how to open my own body up and remove the wound, dress it, treat it. Heal it. I am trying in this process and it is already showing its effects. I can talk about these stories. I can articulate and patch together this *dirty laundry* in ways that relate to larger histories. In ways that give other women goose bumps. Or so they tell me. In ways that don't hurt me so much.

[JULY 2012, RIO DE JANEIRO]

Hitched on a Monday. Celebrated with a beer, a sandwich, and a Lucky. I laugh over the phone with a friend about having a Monday wedding, how there was a lightness to the whole thing. How I needed that lightness in order to marry at all. We didn't have much choice in the matter, not if we wanted to remain in the same country together. This country. The only one of the two between us that will allow our union by law.

X X X X X X X

From the FBI public record of mass shootings in the United States from 2001-2015:
160 incidents total
1,043 casualties
96% of the shooters were male
"Incidents annually" are steadily increasing

"Women worldwide ages 15 through 44 are more likely to die or be maimed because of male violence than because of cancer, malaria, war and traffic accidents combined."

—Nicholas D. Kristof

"Violence is first of all authoritarian. It begins with this premise: I have the right to control you. Murder is the extreme version of that authoritarianism, where the murderer decides he has the right to decide whether you live or die, the ultimate means of controlling someone. . . . A woman is beaten every nine seconds in this country. Just to be clear: not nine minutes, but nine seconds. It's the number-one cause of injury to American women."

—Rebecca Solnit, "The Longest War"

Since age five there has only been one constant: transit. Joint custody, foreign exchange, weekly commutes, a bi-national marriage. I left the home I knew because there were no other options for a girl who picked up the scent of rotting bodies buried in the women around her, who saw despair seething out tiny pores and ragged cuticles, the bloodied carnage piled high from generations before her, around her, closing in. Wasted. All this utterly wasted human capacity and the lethal rage it breeds. The biting perfectionism of the frustrated woman. The broken women who break babies the way they break mustangs. At twelve, I signed a pact in blood with momma, swearing

I would not marry or have babies. It was a pact with myself to remain human. At the first chance: a high school exchange program in Colima, Mexico. Free, except for airfare. Only two students per semester in a school of three thousand. I applied. Anywhere. Anywhere but here. I saved money for the ticket from an afterschool job. I was sixteen. Because the violence of gendering was not taken seriously, I could not call myself a refugee. I could only say: Mexico, New Mexico, Arizona, Madrid, Sacramento, Chicago, New York, Brasília, Rio. I could only see my smiling white face on billboards across Mexico advertising the elite school I attended for free in the exchange. I could only say: I was lucky enough to get away.

—

2001, ST. LOUIS UNIVERSITY, MADRID CAMPUS: I made it to college. I read Alice Walker's recollection of three gifts her mother gave her when she left home and went off to study. Today I only remember one gift—a sewing machine—and the rationale for it: that it was the one tool she could use to make anything she needed so she wouldn't have to depend on anyone else. It stuck with me: the image of that sewing machine being part of feminist theory in an academia in which I felt so alien. I spent a day and a night in that basement apartment scrubbing the tile walls of their years layered in oil spatters, and in those hours, instead of the familiar shame, I felt proud of my mothers, my grandmothers, my aunts. Of the practical skills they had gifted me. Of all they could give.

In 1973, The National Geographic Society conducted an anthropological survey of American Mountain People and concluded that:

> . . . bonds of community have generally been strong and those of family stronger still. Clan solidarity, and the tendency to feelings to be intense when concentrated on relatively few other people, gave rise to the notorious mountain feuds. . . . But it was not because the participants were what we would normally consider murderers, not that they were antisocial, but rather that human bonds counted so much with them—and that they were fiercely independent, impulsive, and fearless.

2003, CALIFORNIA STATE UNIVERSITY, SACRAMENTO: I walk South across campus, past the Edward Rivera mural, past the sites of Esteban Villa's many whitewashed ones, past the English classes in session in Calaveras Hall and the Department of World Languages & Literatures in Mariposa, on my way to meet with the head of Ethnic Studies in search of a signature. I have designed a special major in Chicano/Latino Literature & Art, and I must convince six tenured instructors and four heads of departments that its pursuit is a legitimate one. I must convince the rhetoric instructor that it is not the novelty of an assumed cultural "other" that I find engaging, but the histories and articulations of rural, working class, and Far West experience otherwise absent in academia. I write proposals for a final panel that articulate why I feel moved to resist the dominant narrative that claims culture only travels East to West, North to South, why I wish to study the extensive influences Indigenous America and Africa have had on U.S. and European cultures. In my meeting with the poetry professor, I illustrate my point with the fact that country & western ballads are just boleros sung sideways, and that cowboys are just adaptations of vaqueros. I make my case against the cultural hegemony of an English major. A friend teases me for creating more work for myself. A Film Studies instructor warns me that such a degree will be useless, and then tries to convince me to major in film. Finally, I earn permission to focus my studies on the ancient civilizations of this land, the Silk Road and the Islamic Empire, how Africa made its way through Portugal and Spain and into the so-called New World in ways our national narrative does not allow. I can choose from a selection of literature classes in the English and Spanish Departments, alongside course offerings in History and Art and Sociology that interrogate the undocumented intermixing within our One Drop heritage, and the ways languages change and adapt just as readily as cultures, even in spite of an institutionalized racism set on keeping us segregated.

On the weekend after my petition is approved, I travel back up the hill and stay with the uncle and aunt who raised me. He tells trucking stories while we tend a burn pile. She and I cook dinner. She tells me she prefers the term blended to Eurasian, and we use the language of Chicanismo to talk about our family: my Dust Bowl kin who call themselves White who were once High Germans who lie about Gypsies who marry poor Mexicans who marry poor Swedes who marry poor French Canadians who lie about any kind of Indian who marry poor Nicaraguans who marry poor Blacks who marry poor Blackfeet who marry elite Japanese who marry wealthy Englishmen who marry whomever the fuck they please. It is in the artful overlaps and blending, in the mestizaje, that I feel most at home.

[18 SEPTEMBER 2013, RIO DE JANEIRO]
Pregnant today with this patchwork after last night's Loretta Lynn biopic with my sweetie, sorting laundry, making oatmeal, feeding the plants, changing light bulbs. Now, sitting down to write: nothing. This piece takes place in the body, in the doing. In the body memory of domestic work.

Loretta The Girl Child married, having babies. Loretta The Young Woman spurred to sing professionally by her husband. This is not a common story. No wonder 1980s Hollywood and Nashville wanted to wave it around like an exemplary life. Stand by your man *and* be a professional woman. You *can* have it all. Just don't educate yourself, don't get above your raising, and don't, do not, go at this alone.

-

1992, NEVADA COUNTY, CALIFORNIA: Grandma dresses me in a button-down shirt, pressed with starch, dried by the fireside. She talks me through the binding of a tie, pointed at the end like my father's, knotted perfect. *Don't you never kiss no man's foot.*

-

[NOVEMBER 2013, RIO DE JANEIRO]
I envision burning this quilt in a field as a creative act, the act of destruction. To make a silence. By choice and in healing, not by shame. A friend says, "don't do it." But sometimes the most real part of making work is being able to unthread, to *kill your darlings*, to burn what no longer needs becoming. But perhaps, in this case, it is just the part of me that wants to banish pain.

/ / / / / / /

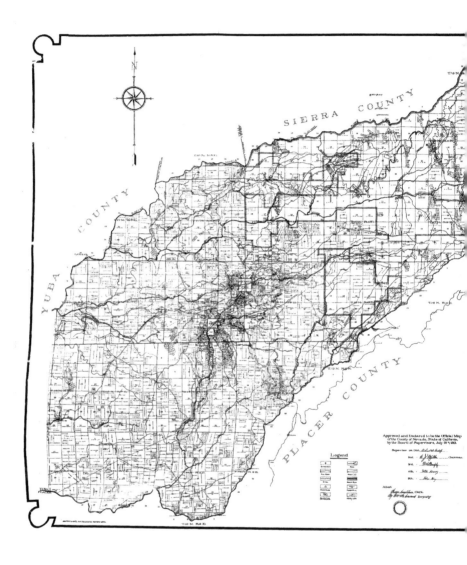

SIERRA COUNTY

PLACER COUNTY

NEVADA COUNTY

CALIFORNIA

OFFICIAL MAP

Compiled by

Fred. M. Miller, County Surveyor

and

Pierce-Bosquit Abstract & Title Co.

Gerald K. Essex. Del.

Scale

Ownership checked to May 1st, 1913.

1949, NEVADA COUNTY, CALIFORNIA: Slaughtering the hogs and tending pregnant sows, she dreams of lace curtains and plush drawing rooms like the ones in the mansion she polishes. She imagines delicate lace gloves covering her wrists, peach parasols and intricate carvings on a lipstick tube, gentle men who drink only when fashionable. But she is fifteen and she is married, and no gentle man would ever have her now. She squeezes down milk from swollen udders, scrapes off foam. She hears him holler, now in from the woods, whiskey thick. He is ready for supper, but she was dreaming and he must drink milk. He whines for pasties, so she retrieves from the cupboard a coffee tin filled with lard. This is his luxury: this coffee tin, this lard. She peels potatoes and sets them to boil, pounds venison from yesterday's kill. Chopping onions, she lets drop tears full of curtsies, of delicate tiny hands being lifted, kissed by a stranger. She rolls out the flour mixture, remembers she is trash. She serves his meal retrieved from oven and pulls out a rag to clean.

If you trace the county lines, ink will outline the shape of a pistol. Teachers at the Catholic middle school and public high school taught this, proud of the coincidence or finding it funny. It's a shape local organizations use to advertise on tote bags and bumper stickers. College professors, meanwhile, taught California Gold Country as the site of the most violent chapter in Native American history.

At the Rough and Ready Succession Days celebration, Grandma orders hot dogs for Grandpa, me, and herself. We sit at a picnic table in front of the VFD and talk to a woman in a handmade bonnet and an old man in plaid. They come every year, she tells Grandma, who fills conversation lulls like she's packing cement. The couple narrates the lineup of events, says that the hanging will start soon. And sure as shit, a scarecrow dressed as a citified Easterner is hoisted up on a rope and left to dangle in the dry summer wind above whoops and hollers. Grandma daintily nibbles at her hot dog, but polishes off a bag of potato chips and orders dessert, "for the two of us to share." Grandpa stares at the rope. He stares off a lot now. We are told to call it Dementia.

The best of the old ways, I told myself, do not die, and especially in the mountains, where people seem to have an extra measure of appreciation for the past. Perhaps this is true in a particular way in the Far West, settled much later than the Appalachians, and the Ozarks. Many western families are only one or two generations removed from the region's first pioneers.

In much of the western mountain country the opportunists have come and gone, taking the wealth of furs, minerals, and timber with them. It is the patient people who remain; steady and independent, they seem to care little for wealth, and see no lasting gain in the pace that exploitation demands. They do

46

1997, NEVADA COUNTY, CALIFORNIA: Lodges offer protection from the elements—Masons, Elks—because the elements always require protecting from. Old loggers sit at café diners, talk about the woods and watch waitresses pass from underneath trucker caps. Denim shirts with filthy cuffs, these forests are for stripping. A bumper sticker: *Paper products no longer available. Wipe your ass with a spotted owl.* Environment versus eating. Humans versus something. Fifteen feet of sediment to prove our versus is stronger than dirt. Name the site Diggins. Hydraulic mining hollows out gorges for gold flakes extracted from where riverbeds once ran. Discolored veins, petrified layers diverted to flumes. Water moves into valleys. Water where history starts with a place name. Malakoff, where the moon beats blue jagged off cliff sides, copper rings on the tips of hoses burning centuries in a midnight glow. Lips wet with hunger. Sluices flood. Miners washed down mountains worth more than extraction. Aching white banks near beds of colorless gravel are speckled with Manzanitas and the Douglas Firs loggers bring home in winter. They hang trinkets from live branches to enact tribal rituals now called Christian. Somewhere in our sediment we remember, blasted, bleeding. Somewhere red clay covers these wounds as salve.

Fifteen feet of sediment at Greenhorn Creek. Fifteen decades slide down cliffs. A yellow Chevy with KC lights cuts clearings through the pines. 4x-ing tires irk up rubble mounds, lose grip, slide back.

Redheaded boys laugh, untwist the caps off forties. Skinny girls in tight sweaters adorn pick-up cabs while stocky girls with round faces giggle across a campfire. Hand-rolled cigarettes and a bong round—celebratory hashish, purple kush. Puff, puff, give. Little girls with broken feathers and gold stains upon their teeth skinny dip in what is left of the water.

The children of hippies and rednecks and shroom-growing neuro-surgeons gather in a city plot on Friday nights to recite Beowulf lines, role play scenes from a vampire story. Their pale, white-powdered faces illuminate the park. Beethoven's Ninth Symphony washes through the trees, and a troubled youth recites a poem he has composed about moonlight and death and longing. He will star in the high school play this fall, and all the girls with purple-painted lips and safety pins in their eyebrows are planning to attend. One boy makes a portrait of each in dotted ink after dropping tabs. Each way you turn the sheet, he says, there is a different image. One girl watched her father's murder when she was eight—quiet, from beneath the bed. In pencil, she sketches the boots of the Hell's Angels she remembers.

Someone's drunken uncle lights up outside the Crazy Horse Saloon. Down Main Street storefronts stand erect, Western Victorian outlines lit as Hollywood façades that have never seen a camera. Façades that speak in whispers, passing histories behind neon, inventing new ones. A cardboard cutout of the Lakota Chief, decorated with a string of Christmas lights and beer advertisements, is mounted above the dance floor. Feathered headdresses and dusty moccasins line ceiling shelves. Unshaven men and eye-shadowed women tap glasses on the worn oak bar, refusing coasters.

2006, NEVADA COUNTY, CALIFORNIA: In Grandpa's blue Jimmy, we ride through the rust-colored mud of what used to be his property in what used to be the mining town of Sweetland in what used to be Nisenan summer grounds before the miners came. He now runs the water truck and is paid to keep the place up. With my grandfather—a lifetime Elks Lodge member who has logged these hills since before my father was born—I am creating an art piece. My grandfather, who is against art and education and educated women creating art, is helping me. He son-of-a-bitches the radio when they play Willie Nelson. I love Willie, and my friends and I have joked that we would bed him given the chance, but I do not tell my grandfather this. We pull up to the padlocked fence and find a NO TRESSPASSING sign he posted in the seventies with five bullet holes rusted through it. He jumps out and, with a crowbar from the toolbox that is bolted in the flatbed, pries it loose, letting the nails fall around the tree's base. He is leaving traces because he loves finding them himself—old Union coins, arrowheads—and hopes that someday someone will find his.

The sign, strung with the barbed wire my uncle cut from his pasture fence, is hanging in an exhibition today. Over the faded lettering another artist has sketched a naked human and oak trees, and I have written a poem comprised of two stanzas with images referencing Malakoff Diggins and not-so-hippie love. My grandfather will travel to Sacramento, he tells me, to see this piece. To see what I have done with the Kenworth mud flap we hauled in from the shop. He will drive the hour and pay too much for parking and walk with his bad knee into Luna's Café where he will have to ask my grandmother what a lee-quah-doe is, and she will have to read the menu carefully. He will see this because I have found I can take my eyes and turn them homeward. This has something to do with Chicanismo, I think.

2014, NEVADA COUNTY, CALIFORNIA: She has taken to hibernation. Pajamas, curlers, fluffy terrycloth slippers. Cups of Earl Grey. The doing and redoing and undoing and losing of taxes. There are always taxes that need doing and redoing and undoing and losing. And there is always a television blaring.

Her children complain that she doesn't like to go out to eat, that she spends the day in her night shirt. They agree to put her on medication, agree that she'll do much better and, since she won't change her situation, at least she won't be so miserable. She rebels, then refuses. She *worked in a mental ward before and how can her own children betray her like this?*

What she will do is go with me to concerts and plays and sit in uncomfortable chairs at storytelling festivals. I take her to see Mary Youngblood and Alastair Fraser and an Elvis impersonator. I take her to a famous old theatre to see "The Patsy Cline Story" and "A Street Car Named Desire." When the scene blackens and the wife is beaten, screams escape from my grandmother's lungs. Pained, voluminous sighs. People around us take notice, shift in their seats, *ssshhh* her. I ask her if she wants to leave. *No.* Another whimper, more shifting. My gut enflames. I throw warning glances in their direction. Holding my grandmother's arm, I plan a speech about Post-Traumatic Stress Disorder not only being a condition of soldiers in case it comes to that, to interrupting this play to defend this feeling woman. I shrink at the thought of disrespecting the artists, but isn't that part of performance—opening yourself up in real time to experiencing something with others? My grandmother trembles, but still she does not want to leave. I wonder if it's out of politeness or because she needs to see this story end.

No one labels the work of Tennessee Williams "trauma porn;" this label is reserved for women who write stories of survival. Tennessee Williams' plays are True Art; the writings of survivors are deemed unimaginative therapy. Kate Zambreno notes in *Heroines* that when the male writer distorts the stories of the women around him—sometimes using their own words—he is considered creative, a genius (see: F. Scott Fitzgerald, Henry Miller), while the woman who writes herself is still a tragic porn star, a victim to her own victimhood, and *how dare she claim it as literature?!*

[DECEMBER 2015, NEVADA CITY, CALIFORNIA]

The "Walking Tour" brochure I picked up in a shop off Broad Street boasts this tagline:

NEVADA CITY

Where the Past
is Always Present

-

2015, SACRAMENTO: Capitol Public Radio announces the first-ever investigation into the links between mining contaminants released into the environment during the 1850s California Gold Rush and the disproportionately high rates of breast cancer among women now residing in the region.

\\|/ \\|/ \\|/ \\|/ \\|/ \\|/

When she was first married, Grandma worked as a nurse in the Department of Mental Hygiene at DeWitt State Hospital. A former Army base, DeWitt housed overflow patients from other California mental hospitals beginning in 1946. By 1960 it housed over 2,800 patients. Grandma was paid an hourly wage to administer medication, bathe patients, scrub hallways. She tells me that several women she had gone to school with were admitted by their husbands when their husbands wanted to remarry. She tells me there was nothing wrong with these women. She tells me she was almost fired for combing a patient's hair and giving her water. She tells me she was not supposed to touch the *crazies*.

I am told I cannot trust anything my grandmother says.

In the 1970s, Billiemae went to work for the United States Air Force. She finally had her financial freedom, but she never left him. She helped pay to have my teeth straightened, said she wouldn't let anything hold me back and couldn't stand to watch my upper lip catch on my protruding fangs.

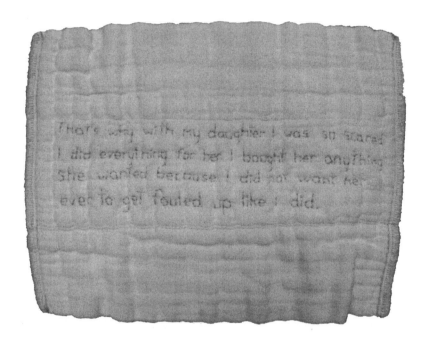

That's why with my daughter I was so scared I did everything for her I bought her anything she wanted because I did not want her ever to get fouled up like I did.

I don't have the right to forget certain things. I think it's a luxury
of our time that should be pressed hard against.
—Dario Robleto

2014, CALIFORNIA: My breast tissues engorge with memory, not milk. I hold my newborn nephew to my chest so my sister may rest, her eyes bleeding a need for sleep. I hold her baby to my body swollen with ancestral heft. My great-grandmother plumping the tissues to welcome new life, her pain spun through helix into nurturing. I carry other bodies in mine for loved ones and for myself. I am not to be mother, always knew this, but keep the maternal lines for those who scrape the cream off milk, hide the blood, trim.

"Crazy quilts, born of necessity, were made in an all-over design consisting of pieces of material, regardless of size or color. With the scarcity of materials in the early days of our country, women cut from worn and discarded woolen clothing any parts that were intact or considered useful. They were sewed together in crazy fashion. . . . In 1870 the lowly crazy pattern was elevated to the parlor by substituting scraps of silks and velvet for the worn woolen pieces."
— Marguerite Ickis, *The Standard Book of Quilt Making and Collecting*

"I find myself in a bind. I'm tired of female pain and also tired of people who are tired of it. I know the 'hurting woman' is a cliché but I also know lots of women who still hurt. I don't like the proposition that female wounds have gotten old; I feel wounded by it."
— Leslie Jamison, "Grand Unified Theory of Female Pain"

"what cannot be said will be wept"
— Sappho

'Contained crazy' is the quilting term used to describe a hodge-podge of pieces stitched together into squares that are then stitched into a larger quilt. Containing crazy seems to be the way handicrafts aim to tame, a pre-determined pattern into which we may filter our wild parts, our worries, our questions, our pain. The women I come from stitch theirs, boil theirs, cut theirs, cover theirs with dirt, and watch, wait for something else to take shape—a shape that has been chosen ahead of time and is anticipated with care. A choice to repeat the past like a refrain in a hymnal, sometimes inspired, sometimes dutiful. A choice to bring the past into their living by not altering its shape or by altering it slightly. This slightness over time allows for a particular continuity, for safety. You always know your position, the extent to which you are needed inside of a unit, hands full of tradition, fingers calloused.

It is family shorthand to call Grandma *crazy*. The screaming, the secrets, the lies, the sneaking of sweet things into hidden places all over the house, into her mouth. The cussing at and blaming of Grandpa for everything. The out-of-breath retellings of the past over and over and over again. Every sentence in a conversation turning to a memory. Her never leaving the house. No one can listen to her for more than an hour or the toxicity begins to infect. Some claim she's made the whole thing up, convinced herself she's the victim when really it's the other way around. They blame her for not leaving, say she slept around. Grandpa can't see why she can't just let the past go. Some worry about him, call how she treats him elder abuse. We see him shrinking. We see her growing large. She considers herself strong in her old age, says she *don't take no more shit*. The rest of us wish there'd have been a divorce long ago, but it's too late. Now, Grandma is crazy because calling her this is easier on us. Pinning it on the woman excuses our own complicity in the normalizing of her pain.

This is what sometimes happens:

The man who is poor and calls himself white beats his wife, gives his money to other women, assures other men who call themselves white of his purity and venom.

The woman who is poor and calls herself Swedish and High German, who is beaten by this man who is poor and calls himself white, calls him *n----r*, reminds him of his kinky hair, that his mother is *i---n*, that his father is, at most, Low German.

These two humans live in a world that offers power in the crushing of another. This world is the one into which many of us are initiated.

2010, RENO, NEVADA: Grandma makes me swear I will never leave her to die in a hospital or a home. She demands I lock her in a cage by the river in Downieville with no food or water. "Once I'm dead, open the cage. I want the wolves to eat me." I tell her this is illegal, but she doesn't pay me any mind. And I don't argue.

[OCTOBER 2012, NEVADA COUNTY, CALIFORNIA]

I buy Grandma books to read in the hospital: a book of myths and a compilation of quotes from Oscar Wilde. She broke her hip pulling weeds in the garden, a chore *Grandpa should've done.* I sit in my car in the parking lot gathering calm before I go in, leafing through the Wilde. I copy down in my notebook: *Selfishness is not living as one wishes to live, it is asking others to live as one wishes to live.*

Grandpa visits her in the hospital every day. He does not say much, just sits in an armchair next to her bed and reads the paper or watches TV. He says this is how his parents loved, always present for one another. Grandma says she wishes he'd go away.

-

[OCTOBER 2012, NEVADA COUNTY, CALIFORNIA]

Grandma in a recovery room listening to Pistol Annies on her headphones, eating grilled cheese, oranges and yogurt. She has woven herself into so many lies, so much hiding and regret that she cannot tear herself from them anymore. It terrorizes. It is sticky and draining. I fear this for myself. I don't want to wake up one day to a gaping hole that is my life.

With lines of women broken on both sides, I wonder if wholeness can ever arise. I did not doubt before that it could, that I would be the one to heal it, but its weight grows heavier as I age.

[OCTOBER 2012, NEVADA COUNTY, CALIFORNIA]

Wake to phone call: "Gram and Gramp are trying to escape the rehab center. They left without signing her out and are planning to drive to L.A. to visit her brother. No one's told her yet that he died."

R and I drive into town, find them trying to start their car in the parking lot. Gram is furious with her family and Gramp is following her orders. I try talking them out of their decision and fail. When I grab for the keys, my eighty-six-year-old grandfather digs his fingers into my arm so tight he draws blood, bruises. I continue to wrestle, piling my weight atop his bony back to pry the keys from his arthritis-curled fingers. There we are: misaligned and warring for the exact same thing.

And there is the woman I am not legally allowed to marry in this country, trying to reach my father on the phone, her voice warbling, holding my grandmother's arm.

-

2012: Last year, the United Nations released the first global report on the human rights of LGBTQ people. This year, Brazil holds rank as home to the most anti-queer murders with 310. The United States comes in second with twenty-five LGBTQ hate-violence homicides and 2,106 incidents reported.

-

2013, RIO DE JANEIRO: The United Nations issues a statement saying that there is no need for Brazil, a democracy, to still maintain its military police force left over from the dictatorship. The government recently employed this force to subdue the millions of protestors in the streets denouncing corruption, cuts to education and municipal infrastructures, attacks on gay rights, and the upcoming World Cup.

R and I march down Presidente Vargas Avenue toward the Governor's Palace with thousands of chanting Cariocas, clapping our hands in unison and feeling safe enough for the first time in our three years here to kiss in public. There is a buoyancy among this mass of humans. Hours pass. We march, sing, chant. I notice metal fencing up ahead on either side of the crowd. We are being corralled.

I am suspicious of corrals, especially those manned by officers wielding assault rifles. It marks me as foreign. R trusts my instincts and follows my urge to fall back. The multi-city protests have remained peaceful so far, but tensions across the country have been mounting, and this is the biggest manifestação yet. We push our way through the singing, through street vendors selling cans of Brahma beer like this is Réveillon because they need the money. And because Brahma is everywhere. Brahma is owned by Ambev. We find the first open metro stop and walk to the second. Something has shifted in the crowd. She senses it now. Two stops and we exit at Glória, walk up the metro stairs, across the cobblestone, ring for the porter, catch the elevator. R checks Midia Ninja on Twitter for updates and tells me the police have fired shots into the crowd we just left, claiming a protester provoked them with a Molotov cocktail. An anonymous Midia Ninja reporter says it was a plant, an excuse to quell this historic, million-strong uprising with the threat of real violence. Several minutes and the streets flood with chanting, the metro vomits protesters. Armed tanks follow close behind hurling "moral bombs" at their heels, into restaurants. History explodes on the uneven streets at the corner of Rua do Catete and Ladeira da Glória, makes our eyes water all the way up on the sixth floor. We rush to slam the doors, push towels and blankets into crevices.

The next day the newsstands are empty. I imagine those same protesters rushing to touch, to purchase a memento of the thing they cannot own: past. I imagine them with their scissors and their cafezinhos cutting away the other headlines, mounting the helicopter photos on the fridge, maybe in a scrapbook or slipped between the pages of a novel. I imagine this as an optimistic act, one done in the *someday I will show my children and my grandchildren a relic from the time I helped change the world, made Brazil better, more livable for them* spirit. I imagine that they imagine how they will tell tales of how bad it was, how hopeless these times seemed until the Revolution of 2013. But perhaps I am overlaying my own experience as an archivist and oral historian. Perhaps these empty newsstands are simply a tribute to some human need to keep a tangible link to the past, a thing we can pick up and touch so as to prove to ourselves that we are here. That we may know, through our body, that other bodies have been here, are still. That we are not without them. That we never have been.

2008, CHICAGO: My cousin loads up her hatchback and drives 409 miles through three states to my apartment while her abuser is away for the weekend on business. She leaves no note, takes the couch she had purchased to a neighbor, and accumulates eight tickets for not having cash on the toll roads. He is 409 miles and three states away now. We spend the days along Lake Michigan walking, biking, talking. We order pizza, watch movies, rest. On the fourth day, we find her car missing. She insists it can't be him. I think, *now he knows where she is, where I live*. I search online to see how easy it is to find my apartment. It takes a few minutes. I thank goodness for the first time in my life for gated apartment buildings, for neighbors so close they can hear everything. I grow angry at the lists of reasons my cousin gives for why it could not have been him. I argue, half joking, "no one else would steal your beater." She smiles. I was with her when she parked her car two blocks away in a spot we both took note of so she could find it again later. A day passes, and the police call to say they have located her car. It has been towed. It was parked six blocks away in the opposite direction in a clearly marked NO PARKING zone. My cousin takes a bus to the tow yard and checks the contents of her car for stolen goods. The cash is still in the cigarette tray, CDs on the back seat. Nothing worth money has been taken, only one item of great sentimental value. Despite all the evidence that keeps piling, my cousin refuses to admit it could only have been him, that this was his best strategy for intimidating her.

She refuses to admit this very real possibility because it means admitting, in her mind, she is somehow weak, and she has never been afforded the luxury to admit such a feeling.

Meanwhile, I am pushing down my rage. This privileged white boy who has tormented my cousin for years, who drives across two states to move her car eight blocks just to intimidate, knows now where I live. My cousin is in danger, I am in danger, and now even my roommate and her cat are at risk, too. One white boy who cannot handle losing his control puts four other beings in danger. Now I am livid. I am desperate and afraid for our lives. I call several women's shelters, but my cousin refuses to go to one, says he'll find her. She wants to go with me to my girlfriend's apartment instead. She needs the warmth of family right now, but I have been broken in these *famili*ar places and try to cut her aching from my body. I think: *I cannot die from this if she will not help herself. I can only do so much.* So I drive her to a motel in another part of the city and we pay the tab in cash under a false name. I park her car many blocks away. I don't sleep, fearing for my cousin's life, fearing I made a mistake. I know the statistics. Most women do. They read: when she tries to leave her abuser, he murders her. I call my cousin, she is talking to her mother on the phone, can she call me back? Her mother doesn't think it could have been him, either. I call my own mother, demand she tell her sister to *PULLHERHEADOUTOFHERASSHERDAUGH-TERISINREALDANGER!* My mother agrees, makes the call, calls me back, assures me I'm doing the right thing.

I lie awake. It tears at me not to be near my cousin, to have drawn boundaries like this. I suspect she feels betrayed. I think for a moment that I made the healthiest decision—*tough love*, we call it. But then I think that, perhaps, I have bought into an individualistic myth that denies our collective responsibility to hold close and protect one another. Perhaps this makes me male-centered, too European. Perhaps my cousin really did know what she needed: human warmth, family. Psychologists tell us that for a person to stop a destructive behavior like abuse, the whole of his or her community needs to condemn it. In other words, an abuser will keep right on abusing unless *everyone* calls him out on it. There need to be consequences, otherwise the abuser will justify his behavior as socially acceptable. And if we have figured out that collective action is required to help the abuser, why not the abused? But it is 2008, and I am awash in ideas of *individual responsibility*. I am convinced that only my cousin can do this for herself.

2008: Artist Tomás Montoya tags me in an image of a recent poster he's made. It bares the word POSTMODERN in large bubbled letters and underneath, in miniscule font, the line: *Western Man's last attempt to put together what never needed to be taken apart.*

Perhaps the tearing apart may not have had to happen in the first place, but language and culture are messy in their constant changing. They are much akin to the piecework of quilting, a technique that sprung from China and was carried across India, Africa and Europe on the Silk Road, adapted and re-envisioned along the way, then carried to the Americas and adapted further by slaves and settlers and those already here. We cannot pretend that we are whole already or disavow our scraps and relegate them to a waste bin in favor of the clean bolts arriving in ships. Postmodernism may be problematic, but we are full of problems. And solutions. We are ripe in our own complicating. We leave a trail of busted needles on the floor from trying to bind seven layers at once.

2014, CALIFORNIA: The old ones pass through my nephew's face, nestle in his skin a lick, get caught in a photograph, a smile, then pass, his face completely changed. We see his parents, an uncle, a grandmother, a great-grandfather, an aunt. Several months in this world and his face begins to settle into its own shape, a new one, with only flecks of light given off by those who came before.

–

My Germanic ancestors deified the life held by trees, gave human intestine as offering for bark.

My grandfathers and uncles logged other hills to keep their houses warm, to fill the bellies of their children.

My parents craft sheets of wood into useful things: kitchen cabinets, dresser drawers, nightstands, towel racks, cutting boards.

I turn pulp into pages, write words on them, print words on them, stitch linen thread between their creases and bind them one to another, make books that fit in the hands.

My rebellion, my turning away, has led me back to a beginning. Not my beginning, but one of the places my human story starts.

My grandfather learned to cook on a ship in the United States Navy. At home, he keeps his oven mitts in a drawer to the left of the electric range, including two his mother quilted from rags he and his brothers once called clothes. The pads are faded and torn, and the batting has come loose, but Grandpa refuses to throw them away. He runs his crooked fingers along the soft, frayed edges when he tells their story. He says his mama still figured out how to sew even after her fingers twisted then fused in place. *Like mine*, he says. *Feel here where a barbed wire fence went clear through to the bone, never healed right.* He takes a moment to admire his own hands, how their hard-fused bones bring his mother close again.

-

2012: Grandma tells me Grandpa insists they subscribe to Oprah's *O Magazine.* "He likes reading the articles," she giggles.

-

In 2015, David J. Morris writes for Slate.com that Post-Traumatic Stress Disorder "afflicts upward of 30 percent of veterans today and is the fourth most common mental health condition in the world."

We say hill folk are a people of song. We think of the Appalachia we see in film.

Tu vida es un musical, says a host mother. She says I have a song for everything, poetry tucked into the lining of my jacket. She points to me to sing in moments of sorrow. This was over a decade ago, when I'd come down off the mountain into a concrete block that forbade stepping on grass. *No pisar el cesped.*

Now broken lines of poems and neurological research fill hems and linings. I shake them out onto paper. Some fall into the trash bin as I tie up the bag. Some slip across the blade of a knife slicing lemon.

Mountain people share a need to be well away from the press of humanity, to keep a buffer of woods or chaparral between them and the throng, to enjoy a sense of space around them. To thrive on separation requires a spiritual self-reliance and hardihood and even, perhaps, a certain solitariness of soul. With this, I believe, goes a bent for craftsmanship, a capacity to be content and absorbed in the practice of the woodsman's arts, the working of clay on a wheel, the pressing of knife or chisel to a smooth, yielding

HERANÇA

In my original artist statement for the first exhibition of this fiber installation during the 2012 ArtRio at Fábrica Bhering in Rio de Janeiro, I wrote:

> MADE WITH is a meditation on domesticity, on the traditions of woman-made crafts and the repetitive acts of stitching, cooking. Here I investigate legacies of domestic violence, war and social upheaval and how their residues are passed from generation to generation in unspoken ways, bound up in the bodily

acts of domestic work. How one can simultaneously love and resent this work and the emotional impact it has on the body. How the very repetitive nature of these acts become a way to process their effects.

This project begins in my own family and extends out to the women across economic and cultural lines in whose kitchens and homes I have lived throughout the past fifteen years.

But before I could lay down words in the shape of complete sentences, there was no other way into this work than through the two mediums I'd given up in adolescence: song and stitch. So I wrestled with them in the way adults do when they take up drawing again at sixty: naïve, wobbly, eager, heartfelt. After earning an MFA in writing, the amateurism was freeing.

BILLIMAE WAS A FIGHTER AND SHE DID THE BEST SHE COULD
DIDN'T CARE IF HER HAIR KEPT A CURL AS SHE RACED ACROSS T
WITH ALL THE LITTLE BOYS WHO ASKED HER TO PLAY DEAD
SHE KEPT ON RUNNIN', PRETENDED NOT TO HEAR A WORD THEY SAID

BILLI KEPT ON RUNNIN', BILLI WANTED TO SEE THE WORLD
BUT SHE GOT MARRIED, HAD THREE BOYS AND A BABY GIRL
SHE'D RUNNED OFF WITH A MAN SHE COULD HARDLY STAND
JUST TO GET AWAY FROM HER STEPDADDY'S WANDRIN' HANDS

IN A LITTLE SHACK ON PINEY WOOD AVENUE
HER OLD MAN LEFT BRUISES EVEN ~~AFTER~~ AS HER BELLY GREW
AND WHEN HE THREW OUT ALL HER RECORDS SHE SCREAMED, NO!
BUT HE STILL MADE HER LISTEN TO HIS COUNTRY RADIO

FOR FIFTY YEARS, BILLI SCRUBBED THAT OL MAN'S LOGGIN' SHIRTS
SHE MADE HIS COFFEE, TRIED TO BURY ALL HER HURT
AS SHE WATCHED HIM DRINK AWAY AGAIN AND AGAIN
ALL THE MONEY FOR THEIR BABY'S OXYGEN

BILLIMAE'S BABIES HEARD HER SONGS AND HER SCREAMS
THEY MEMORIZED THE CHORUS OF HER DREAMS
BUT THE OLDEST, HE COULDN'T MAKE IT IN BILLI'S WORLD
HIS WAS A FIRE THAT REFUSED TO BURN

BILLIMAE TRIED AND TRIED TO LEAVE
SHE GOT ~~HERSELF~~ A JOB AND A TRAILER IN THE CITY
WITHOUT THE BLACK EYES, SHE ~~COULD SEE~~ SAW SHE'S KINDA PRETTY
BUT THAT OLD MAN JUST WOULDN'T LET HER BE

BILLIEAE'S BABIES HEARD HER SONGS AND HER SCREAMS

THEY'VE MEMORIZED THE CHORUS OF HER DREAMS

WOODS   BILLI ~~TRIED TO LEAVE~~ LEFT HIM BUT ALL SHE GOT WAS BLUE

SHE CRIED ALONE INSIDE 'CAUSE NOBODY KNEW

BILLIMAE WAS A FIGHTER AND SHE DID THE BEST SHE COULD

WHEN THE WORST WAS BEHIND HER, SHE TRIED TO DO SOME GOOD

SHE SHOVED ~~TEN~~ TWENTIES IN MY PALM WHEN HE WASN'T ~~LOOKING~~ there

SAID, "THIS IS FOR THEM BOOKS, YOUNG LADY. YOU GET TO YOUR SCHOOLING."

BILLI STILL CRIES AT NIGHT TO ELVIS AND PATSY CLINE,

~~SHE~~ TALKS OF ALL THE TIMES SHE ALMOST MADE IT OUT ALIVE

'IT'S BEEN TOO LONG FOR ME, TOO LONG," SHE SAYS

AND WE BOTH KNOW SHE'S LEFT HERSELF FOR DEAD

BILLIEAE'S BABIES HEARD HER SONGS AND HER SCREAMS

WE'VE MEMORIZED THE CHORUS OF HER DREAMS

I WANTED TO ~~WATCH~~ SEE HER FIGHT, TO SEE HER ~~MAKE IT THROUGH~~ WATCH STRUGGLE FREE

BUT ~~EVERY TIME I TRY~~ SHE REFUSES TO START ANEW NOW

THROUGH THE GHOSTS IN HER YARD SHE JUST COULDN'T SEE

I STILL LISTEN TO BILLI'S COUNTRY RADIO

I LISTEN TO THOSE OLD SONGS, FAST AND SLOW,

SINGING OF HEARTACHE AND HOME AND KEEPING WILD

AND THEY MAKE ME PROUD TO BE BILLI'S FIRST GRANDCHILD

I GOT BILLI'S TEARS IN THE PALM OF MY HANDS

AND I'LL BE DAMNED IF I DON'T DO SOMETHING WITH THEM

I GOT BILLI'S BLOOD RACING THROUGH ~~MY~~ THESE CROOKED VEINS

BLESS HER HEART, I'M GONNA MAKE (A) CHANGE.

THIS STORY

[10 DEZEMBRO 2013, RIO DE JANEIRO]

Sometimes when you feel clean and tired, the laundry breaks
the line.

-

[JUNE 2015, SACRAMENTO]

Words fail here. At the loosening of skin from muscle, bone. At the
horror of layers floating detached in a swill of liquid, sun refracted
from surface. Holding the cold in a closed fist that comes undone like
sugar, reconfigured in a contaminated order, full of plankton and light.

I resist the act of writing to be fully present in my body—stitching, making, moving. This need makes the shaming come alive again: *you are lazy, too feminine, too poor to be smart, too rural. A bumpkin.* But if I keep moving, if I stay in this wordless making, I soak in its power on its own terms. I am released from the peculiar colonization of the written word upon my flesh.

Here comes Stephanie Sauer (sour) ready for a party in her princess style dress. She has chosen a floral print fabric with large pink flowers on an off white background. This close-fitting and flared dress is fully lined with back zipper, elastic shoulder straps, and short, self-lined sleeves. The contrasting bow on each sleeve, hair bow and purse complete her outfit beautifully.

Stephanie is 10 years old. She is in 5th grade at Mount Saint Mary's School and is an honor student. She is in her 2nd year of sewing at Kentucky Flat 4-H club, her other projects include horse,cooking and arts & crafts. Stephanie's hobbies are basketball, dancing, drawing, math, camping and sewing.

 THANK YOU STEPHANIE

4-H-4010

4-H FASHION REVUE EVALUATION

NAME Stephanie Sauer CLUB Kentucky Flat

AGE 10 NUMBER OF YEARS IN CLOTHING PROJECT _____

GARMENT Flowered dress

	Total Appearance — 75%	Needs Improvement	Acceptable	Well Done
TOTAL APPEARANCE	Creative Selection: • occasion • style • color • texture			✓
	Fit: • bodice/top • skirt/pants			✓
	Grooming			✓
	Posture/Poise			✓
	Undergarments (suitable)			✓
	Accessories (if needed)			✓

	Garment — 25%			
GARMENT	Construction • suitability of method used (end result) • grainline • quality of work			✓
	Pressing			✓
	Care (laundered, mended)			✓

COMMENTS: Very pretty party dress. Good job on sleeves & bows. Nice accessories. Good pressing Smile more!

-over-

A memory: the oversized coat my momma made me. No, the one she gave me that she had made for herself. The one that hung large on my child body, the denim one with the fabric patchwork on the back, the one I loved so much because it was magic. It was magic because my momma made it. It was magic until my aunt picked me up from school, ashamed of my oversized homemade hand-me-down, and took me to J. C. Penny's to buy *something new. Something nice.* Something that would make me fit in at the private school for which her mother helped pay tuition. Something that would keep the kids there from calling me trash. *White Trash* had become my nickname at this new school, but I didn't mention this. I loved that jacket. I loved the world it made, the one I could disappear into on the playground I roved alone.

It is this magic I need to keep. It is palpable. It has a taste.

–

[OUTUBRO 2013, BELO HORIZONTE, BRASIL]

This city's Mercado Central is full of nostalgia for the farm, for rural living. Rows and rows of artisan food stalls, tobacco for palha cigarettes, tooled leather, carved wood, limestone and copper ovenware, hats in woven straw and spoons carved from coconut husks. Caged animals, biscoitos, handmade toys, homespun textiles. In a city made up of folks fresh off the ranch in a world where, for the first time in history, more humans live in cities than in the countryside, this palpable nostalgia makes an intuitive kind of sense. My girl and I eat a hearty lunch at a restaurant with a line out the door. I buy things I don't need except in longing. Wooden spoons, mostly.

UNDATED, RIO DE JANEIRO: A friend's mother sees me stitching, pulls out a tea towel she embroidered for her daughter, tells me, *especialmente com filhas, costurar é terapía. Especially when you have daughters, sewing is therapy.* But sometimes there is more rage than can be soothed by a stitch.

-

[SEPTEMBER 2013, RIO DE JANEIRO]

We settle on *Herança* as the Portuguese title of this quilt installation in the upcoming ArtRio show. *Inheritance.* Not a literal translation, but more exact in her tongue.

Two weeks non-stop work on the installation until late at night in the factory. Eating canned tuna and bread. Green tea, black tea, coffee. Loretta Lynn, Billie Holiday, and Bobbie Gentry playing. *Harper Valley PTA* and 90s Reba on repeat. Difficult, bitter, satisfying days. A quebracabeças with the patchwork on a table that is not quite big enough to fit a queen-size sheet for measuring. Nowhere to measure. Much guesswork. Making do: my strength. Not being able to follow a pattern well coming in handy in having to make this up.

-

Another artist from the factory visits my studio before ArtRio begins. When she sees the installation, the quilt, her eyes glass. The headboard I salvaged from the dumpster was her grandfather's, she tells me.

Visitors to this installation ask if I am from the South of Brazil when they see the photograph on the wall, until they notice the air conditioner in the background.

Needle on the machine breaks. I bought the wrong thread. Too thick. Nowhere to buy needles in this neighborhood, and I can't afford the time to travel to another. Exhibit deadlines. I find a seamstress in her atelier down the hall who has four extras. She won't accept money, so I gift her a vintage sewing pattern I picked up in a thrift store back home, something she eyed when she saw the quilt. We swap stories. She shows me her work for sale and the misprinted Disney fabrics she found at the outdoor Saara market. She is especially proud of an Indian version with Mickey rendered as a kind of Hindu god. She inspects my work for technical precision and for materials she recognizes or finds novel.

ALDEAS FLAMENGAS FAZENDO RENDA

A feitura de rendas tem sido, já de muito tempo, uma das principais indústrias domésticas da Bélgica, e em várias aldeias e pequenas cidades vemos grupos de mulheres nas portas de suas casas movendo àgilmente as agulhas e os bilros. Fazem rendas primorosas e às vêzes de grande valor artístico.

1971

[SETEMBRO 2013, RIO DE JANEIRO]

These city girls from São Paulo and Rio remind me I'm roughshod. They come so polished, so clean at the hem. Their generations and generations of preening reveal me fresh off the farm, the straw still stuck between my teeth.

People walk into the installation and ask if this is a sewing atelier, if I make bedspreads to sell, if I am a seamstress, if I teach quilting workshops. And it strikes a nerve that using a historically feminine medium still automatically deems this piece *craft* and not *art*. I am suspect of those distinctions, but still irate at this continuous treatment of my work as something not to be considered more carefully because it is aligned with this history. Still. This is the second year of the VIDA Count, an independent poll of prominent U.S. publications that has revealed extreme systematic discrimination against women who write. Offenders claim that the culprits for our lack of inclusion are *what* women write and *how*. Still.

A retired seamstress visits. She stands for several minutes in front of the quilt, inspecting, reading. She asks me to talk about the piece. I speak of the impact of all we inherit, the stories, the memories of bruised flesh and broken lives, the love, the skills, the scarring. She nods in consideration. She thanks me for this work. She says it is *important*, then leaves.

She comes back an hour later with her mother.

[6 August 2014, Sacramento]

A traveling exhibition of quilts is on display at the Crocker Art Museum. The community room houses an 1880's 'crazy' quilt-in-progress made by Lydia E. Hayes Leeds. Velvets and satins mounted on paper—old mailing envelopes, handwritten letters.

The exhibition committee underestimated public interest in this traveling exhibition and did not print enough catalogs.

-

[November 2014, Nevada City, California]

Waitress with a voice so sticky sweet it makes me want to lash out, throw things, expel the rage she was penning. The grating sugar crystals hill women layer upon their speech, deftly shaping voice into confectionary slices so seemingly content to put others at ease. I know this voice. I hear it spill out of my own mouth sometimes. It is the other side of a rage like Grandma's. It is with this dusting of sugar that the throat closes.

-

[2014, Rio de Janeiro (gig) ⇒ miama (mia)]

To cut out, cut down to the bone. To cut into the heart and repair the damage.

> "You repair the thing until you remake it completely."
> —Louise Bourgeois

Don't never let nobody call you Okie. Until college I spelled it "Oakie" and thought my Grandma's advice had something to do with the fact that my parents were cabinet makers.

-

HOW DOES A HILLBILLY LET HERSELF BE AN ARTIST?

1. Listen to the mountains the rivers the rocks the trees the spiders the people.

2. Get the hell out of the mountains.

3. Learn to speak at least two other languages so as to trace the ways your own tongue limits you. See the ways you speak more freely in these sounds that are new to you.

4. Take up forms of making that have no practical use. Devour these. Hone these. Exteriorize. Repeat.

5. Stay the hell out of the mountains.

6. Allow yourself to sulk in your disgust of city life and the strangeness of city folk.

7. Allow yourself to be surprised by and admit to your newfound love of city life and city folk.

8. When ready, go into the hell that was the mountains. Spend time working in, playing in, making in the site of the attempted pillage of your throat. Spend the time you need.

9. Keep speaking until the larynx grows stronger.

10. Brave your pain. Bite down on your knuckles, if need be.

11. Snap back. Protect what you've made. Take notice of the parts of you that are no longer broken. The larynx is strong and sounds like it did—no, stronger than it did—at the time before it started warping.

_ | _ | _ | _ | _ | _ | _ | _

As I write these passages, I silence myself. I doubt what I have to say because I anticipate that all it will be met with is doubt. If the arts are part of a larger cultural conversation, I still don't feel entitled to participate in this conversation. Writing is a battleground between compulsion and necessity. The compulsion to *shut up and sit pretty.* Still.

It was not until age thirty that I could write in first person plural. It was not until age thirty that I felt entitled enough to write using the word "we," to claim myself as part of a larger cultural conversation.

I have so much to say but cannot say it. Not in any coherent, essayistic way. Part silence, part censored and disapproved, part panicking about not being *expansive* enough as a woman writing. And so I doubt. I turn toward sewing, toward the underworld work, the invisible, devalued, decorative arts that code all the things I have no room to speak.

94

I grew fascinated with language because language was the thing used to contain me, to beat me into smaller and smaller pieces so that I would be easier for my family and my culture to stomach. So I studied the words, the syntaxes. I kept a spiral notebook where I composed rhyming poems, copied down strings of letters I liked the sounds of but didn't understand. I looked up their definitions. I made lists from a thesaurus of words to use in future rhyming poems. I turned to paper when punished for speaking. Dish soap and thumbs down my throat. *Be seen, not heard. Be accommodating and sweet.* I was told terrible stories about myself, explanations for why I was so strange, so troublesome and mean. I became a bully who was bullied. I had no other way to say things. *Bad words* were off-limits, but bad words turn toxic when kept inside a body. They eat away at the esophagus, erode the trachea.

I notice I have taken to yelling in the streets like most Cariocas. If someone wrongs me, I say so. I shout it, if need be. If the bus threatens not to stop even when my arms are clearly signaling, I step out into the street and flail them, pound on the siding, if necessary. I've become insistent. I've become louder here than I was in my first country, too, in moments of joy, not just anger. I share a big laugh with a stranger at the suco stand and strike up a quick dialogue with the guy selling roscas along Rua da Gloria. I notice the city as wrapped in an ongoing conversation fueled by heat—that of acknowledging each other.

At first, I do not recognize the impulse to partake as me. I just like how it feels in the body. It begins at home, where I learn how to fight with my spouse. We did not fight in my family. We learned not to raise our voices, to instead ice each other out when angry, to stay silent for days or weeks or years. To hold it all in and not give one another the benefit of our honesty. We disowned—the most violent rejection, the opposite of holding. The opposite of love. We were, most of us, afraid to repeat the violence we'd seen in the generations before us. We did not know to distinguish between the violent fight and the connecting one. We thought them all the same. With R, I have to learn this art. It is messy at first, and I do not understand where the limits are, but slowly I learn to expel the things that hurt, the things I need her to see. It takes years, but I finally grasp that I will not be cut away. From this knowing, I learn to speak. And I learn to hear. The difference between Brazilians and United Statesians, between those raised to appear male and those raised to appear female, it seems, has something to do with the way words are held and released.

It is strange to use text in this quilt—that is, to employ written language in a tradition developed largely by silenced ones: the slave, the wife, the woman. But this is my reality now: writing, the privilege of my education. This is my contribution to the tradition, then. An expansion, not a breaking.

Bringing quilting into writing, integrating it: the only way this work is real. For it to exist only as Roman script on white paper would be a false making, a forced sterilization.

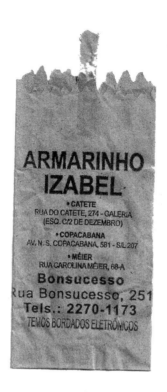

On paper, I cannot move my pen in a straight line. I have tried and it is terrible. Some would say good, but I don't believe them. Things move *sidewards*. Lines round, contain too many hyphens, rests, commas, internal rhymes, refrains.

I am unable to fill in the ligaments. I am working with bones and a superficial filling would be untrue.

In quilting, the up-front work is gathering and cutting and piecing separate scraps, laying them side by side without connection. Moving them around until a pattern emerges. Only later does the binding happen, the stitches that make of these patches a whole, and an older quilt becomes its batting. The binding, here, requires a collaborative effort. The writing, the reading, the patching.

It is best to listen to Zora Neale Hurston and Jeanette Winterson read aloud while stitching.

Hurston, as read by Ruby Dee: "I'm stone deaf from standing still and trying to smile."

[The unhealthy tendency of unembodied words on a page.]

It is the compulsion of the Western fine art tradition to break from that very tradition. We call this Innovation and True Art and deny that it came from anything but Pure Genius. We are often blind to the continuity, even the continuity of the impulse to *make it new*.

In my lecture slides, I use Victorian crazy quilts and Sheila Pepe's installations, Sheila Hicks' individual works to visually explore these ideas...

* DISRUPTIVE

EXCESS *

They are the images that come to mind for me and my attempt to connect this rhetoric to a handful of young visual artists.

" THIS 'STYLE,' OR 'WRITING,' OF WOMEN TENDS TO PUT THE TORCH TO FETISH WORDS, PROPER TERMS, WELL-CONSTRUCTED FORMS. THIS 'STYLE' DOES NOT PRIVILEGE SIGHT; INSTEAD, IT TAKES EACH FIGURE BACK TO ITS SOURCE, WHICH IS AMONG OTHER THINGS TACTILE. "

SWEEP PORCH, HANG LAUNDRY, WIPE COUNTERS, MAKE ICED TEA, WATER PLANTS, SWIM, WATCH THE MOON A WHILE.

Insomnia, thinking of Rachel. our baby, my regret, anger. Heartsore. Healing. Slowly.

LUCE IRIGARAY

'THE POWER OF DISCOURSE AND THE SUBORDINATION OF THE FEMININE.'

" THE ARTICULATION OF THE REALITY OF MY SEX IS IMPOSSIBLE IN DISCOURSE, AND FOR A STRUCTURAL, EIDETIC REASON. MY SEX IS REMOVED, AT LEAST AS THE PROPERTY OF A SUBJECT,

SIGHT = associated with the male desire to see things clearly and logically and to master them theoretically.

FROM THE PREDICTIVE MECHANISM THAT ASSURES DISCURSIVE COHERENCE. "

IRIGARY IN NELSON (38)

class gives more attention to the diary and the ways women have written their lives to capture their personal, social, and historical circumstances.

An examination of the ongoing critical conversation about the nature of women's autobiography is useful in understanding the contexts in which *Inscribing the Daily* appears. During the past fifteen years, feminist critical assessments of women's autobiography have focused, first, on the kinds of narratives women have told and second, on the ways in which such narratives inscribe the self. Both approaches suggest ways in which diary scholarship enters the autobiographical debate by emphasizing the narrative content, structure, and self-presentation of women's writing. In her introduction to *Women's Autobiography: Essays in Criticism* (1980), Estelle Jelinek suggests that women's autobiography is characterized by irregularity, discontinuity, and fragmentation rather than a coherent shaping of life events (17–19). In *The Female Autograph* (1984), Domna Stanton foregrounds women's self-inscription and recognizes that race and class as well as gender need to be addressed in analyses of women's autobiographies. Later, in *The Tradition of Women's Autobiography: From Antiquity to the Present* (1986) Jelinek argues that the episodic, anecdotal, nonchronological and disjunctive style of women's autobiographical tradition is characterized by a "multidimensional, fragmented self-image" yet also by a "self-confidence and a positive sense of accomplishment in having overcome many obstacles to their success" (xiii). Based on her observations, Jelinek calls for a reevaluation of the criteria for autobiography criticism; and this call suggests that the special narrative qualities of the diary and their place within women's writing are important as critics reconsider the structures, the politics, and the context of life writing.

Cannot shake this anger at the tearing down of things I've made. The lives.

Began appliquéing scraps of fabric from the unfinished quilt I started at thirteen with my mother. Found the box in an old shed behind Grandma's house. Had to clean rat shit off the top, but the contents were good. I am following the need to stitch our brokenness, all my brokenness into this quilt. But I still don't trust healing as possible.

- - - - - - - - - - - - - - - - -

I know I cannot be the first woman to turn to quilting as suture. I stop in at a used bookstore to search for others, find these words in Dr. Gladys-Marie Fy's Preface to *Stitched from the Soul: Slave Quilts from the Ante-Bellum South*:

> of the stitching pattern; the relative length and evenness reflect a certain amount of inner harmony. Deviations from this pattern might well indicate that the quilt maker was nursing physical and emotional wounds. Color preferences and abrupt changes in design might also serve as indicators of general well-being.
>
> Additional physical clues might be stains from tears or blood. All of these clues help us trace the life cycles of individual slave women, as well as chart their experiences and the knowledge they gained along the way.
>
> In a sense, the stitches, the tears, and the blood are "time markers" of the everyday events in their lives: marriages, births of children, illnesses, separation of family members by sale or death, whippings, punishment, deprivation, and so forth.
>
> Denied the opportunity to read or write, slave women quilted their diaries, creating permanent but unwritten records of events large and small, of pain and loss, of triumph and tragedy in their lives. And each piece of cloth became the focal point of a remembered past.

I buy the book. I underline, highlight, circle passages. I write notes in pencil in the margins about quilting bees being a type of consciousness-raising circle. I write questions, too. I keep searching. I find entire histories of silent, layered narratives like the ones in Harriet Powers' metered blocks. I read about the ancient languages that were imbued with new meaning and embedded in Freedom Quilts, hung out in plain view to signal the way toward safe passage out of the South.

I find a kind of kinship in the reprinted patterns, their textures and staining, the merely decades-old but extensive scholarship on the subject. Until reading Fry's words that day in the bookstore, I had never intellectualized quilts. I had only stitched my way toward them. I had studied the prosody at work in Adrienne Rich's "Aunt Jennifer's Tigers," but never the stitching itself. I could not think about stitching; knowing is all tied up in motion and bleeding. I had to just make holes, bind layers, rips seams back out, prick my skin. Start over. See perfection in the lack of it.

Education, I find, has less to do with knowing things and more to do with the crafting and recrafting of onself.

-

I begin sewing a welcoming quilt for my new nephew from scraps of worn-in family clothing. Sometimes we must make a thing only for our love of the person receiving it. I am pulled to make him something to touch, something to hold over his little boy body when it feels fragile or alone or battered by the world, something to remind him he is loved. Something to protect him from the particular brutality this world holds for his little boy body.

The making of his quilt takes months away from my studio practice, places me in the bedroom with a fold-up table, sewing machine, chair. I love this making. It returns me. Yet I cannot help but feel plagued by the notion that turning my making toward a loved one minimizes my work, places me back in the world of country crafts and women's work—quilts, scrapbooks, embroidery. I have swallowed the myth of male genius, too, despite my body's attempts to reject it. It poisons my love of other ways of making, insisting that I am less of an artist when I care for those around me.

I refuse this. I see all around me a world of makers, many of them women, equally adept at committing to their own making *and* at elevating those around them. I slash open a vein to drain the poison. I suck out the altered blood and spit mouthfuls on the ground. I cauterize the breakage, begin interviewing makers who also make space for others. I make plans to publish a series of these interviews, then a book.

In their most active years, members of the Royal Chicano Air Force—originally called the Rebel Chicano Art Front—did not distinguish between those who secured the grants, organized the events, prepared food, repaired the engines, and those who made the artwork. This act of denying divisions was a conscious subversion of Eurocentric frameworks of art and life and culture. Or, as Dr. Ella Maria Diaz explains, "An important component of the RCAF's creation of a Chicano/a mural environment was their collapse of artistic hierarchy in opposition to the idea of beauty and artistic genius as the realm of the individual artist." In the tellings and retellings of their story in the popular press, however, this ideology is downplayed, and the more conventional story of the RCAF as a core group of visual artists becomes History.

Arthur Bispo do Rosário stitched for himself the *Manto da Apresentação*, an Afro-Brazilian mantle in which he would present himself to his Creator. He made it from the threads of blankets and blue uniforms he wore as a patient at the Colônia Juliano. He embroidered into the cover of this mantle words that came to him in visions, names of those he "would save and take to the new world." He spent his lifetime stitching this piece of textile that would serve, for him, a much higher purpose upon death. He meant to wear this piece into the next world.

But Bispo do Rosário was not buried in his mantle. His mantle hangs instead in a museum at the São Paulo Biennale where I view it on display. His mantle is now Art, extracted from the sacred purpose with which he had imbued it. Bispo do Rosário is now hailed as one of the most important artists and visionaries of the twentieth century, but he had no say in this matter of his mantle. Bispo do Rosário was *crazy*.

Can the care of others alter our epigenetics? Can tenderness clear away the stuff history fixes to our more ancient deoxyribonucleic acid? Can the blood that pulses through those who show us love extend into our own veins? Can it reconfigure damage already done? Does our blood begin to mirror theirs the way our brains do when we empathize? In the child taken in by nurturing aunts, uncles, grand-, and adoptive parents, can the helix be scrubbed clean of its ancestral detritus? Affection can fill out the coral fans that extend from the bases of our brains and build up our immunities, but what of the blood? Can our own love for others change their biology?

-

Country songs that give voice to domestic violence follow the trope spelled out in Carrie Underwood's rendition of "Blown Away": "Daddy was a mean old mister / momma was an angel in the ground." But Grandma is no angel. Coming to understand this does not wipe clean the past or justify a single act committed by her mean old mister. It simply allows me to love two other humans more fully. It also does something to the stories I tell myself in order to live.

-

Eeyore has a Facebook page with 3,683,284 followers.

-

Nine of Billboard's Top 100 Country Songs of 2014 were about numbing. They are:

96. Rum
88. Drinking Class
65. Drunk Last Night
34. Day Drinking
17. Drink to That All Night
11. Drink a Beer
8. Drunk on a Plane
7. Bartender
4. Bottoms Up

-

[JANUARY 2015, NEVADA COUNTY, CALIFORNIA]

Today: skinny dipped. alive, finally.

Today: woke at five and answered questions for an interview. solid first draft, needs editing.

Today: visited my uncle. he hurt himself piling wood while i was sick.

Today: "The way to get unstuck is to get stucker for a while."

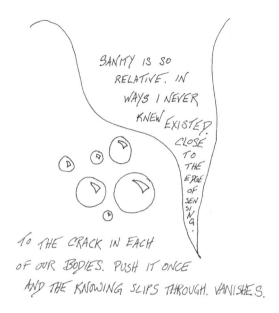

SANITY IS SO RELATIVE. IN WAYS I NEVER KNEW EXISTED. CLOSE TO THE EDGE OF SENSING. To THE CRACK IN EACH OF OUR BODIES. PUSH IT ONCE AND THE KNOWING SLIPS THROUGH. VANISHES.

[6 MARCH 2015, SACRAMENTO]

Deep into the waste. Down around aright in the gentle. Just in the gentle. Cut it off there. Let it aplenty. Flush out the common cold with a splash of honey. Dive into the fire and flesh it out—all the blocked arteries and hard edges. Bask in it. Flip it over. Toss it in the heat. Burn. Burn it up higher. A white heat. Burn. Raise it up.

Brazil signed into law a bill that provides strict penalties for female homicide, or *femicide*. Newspapers cite the high numbers of murders of wives and girlfriends in homes across the country.

How have I never heard the term *femicide* used in relation to domestic abuse murders and not only to drug-cartel crimes in Juárez? Our language, until recently, has never fully reflected the gravity of violence against women. *Violence against women.* Even this terminology has lost its power.

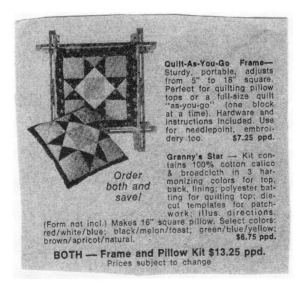

I put language to a thing and all of a sudden it feels valid, clarified, given weight. It stops haunting me in its insistence to be heard, voiced. It finds solace in articulation. This happened in college with the phrase *marital rape*. I am not the first one to figure out this power

III

in naming, but I am taught by male example not to reference facts like these, not to point to a cultural past since such a gesture is to present oneself as unoriginal when the Western ideal of Art is originality. But there is nothing original about any of this human becoming. There is nothing original about the sequencing of words on a page, in the mouth. To deny these genealogies, to absorb them without honoring them first is an act of cowardice, a fragility I cannot respect. Far worse than cannibalism: parasitic.

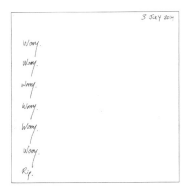 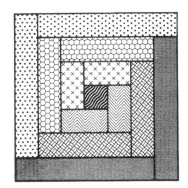

At DeWitt State Hospital in the ward in which my grandmother worked, lesbians were held. *Held*: a couched term for institutionalized. Back when queer was pathological. Back then is not back. It takes me seven years to tell my grandmother I am married to a woman. "Do you think I am some kind of prude?" she snaps. "No, Gram, I just didn't want you to get beat when Gramp found out or live with the fear that he would."

-

[APRIL 2014, SACRAMENTO:]

Recommendations:
Fish oil containing 1000mg each EPA & DHA
50mg 5HTP twice daily
900-1800mg St. John's Wart
Or: a pharmaceutical SSRI
Exercise, sauerkraut, yogurt, lemon balm, coffee.

I laugh at the notion that we always eventually become the thing we hate so we can learn to love it. I do not love this yet. I have stripped myself of shame and sunk into resentment, loathing, anger, fear. Oh, and laziness—the cardinal sin of my culture. Two doctors diagnose me with Major Depressive Disorder. They say it tends to run in families. I would never have said Depression ran in my family, only tears and heart disease and diabetes. Depression was not a language I used even when fantasizing my own death inside a life I had crafted with love. There was no sense to its onset, but I let myself fall. I crawled inside its dampness. If I were to use the term, I would say the Depression in my family tends toward the working kind: you rise out of bed early each day and bite back your pain until the flesh grows brittle. Until it breaks you or you break someone else. I didn't want shame to prop me up, so I kicked it out from underneath me. I want my leanings to be kept in check by love, the kind of love that has never been afforded to the women (or the men?) in my family. A kind of love that is rarely afforded to women at all, anywhere. I didn't want to keep hobbling around, propping myself up with shame and loathing and supplanted love. I wanted it in me, damn it. And so I kicked.

"In my language, we have no word for depression. Instead we say: the heart is spoiled, like milk."

Milk does not unspoil, but my mother has begun to make kefir from milk that is just that, essentially. After she asked the doctors to cut out her cancer-riddled ovaries, she overhauled her diet. She sends me home with a mason jar full of bacteria and lactose with instructions to leave it sit out on my counter for three days and then drink. It is more nutritious, scientists say. It is good for the gut, and studies have shown gut health to be linked to Major Depressive Disorder. Healing calls for nutrients once in abundance in my ancestors' diets:

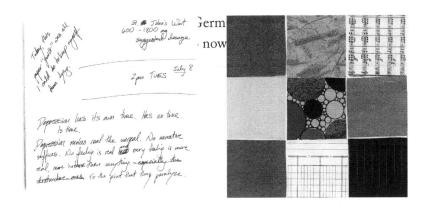

2014: Made sixteen jars of marmalade today from the lemons on my cousin's tree. All failed to set up. Batch was too large, then I over-cooked it in an attempt to force its setting.

I make lemon pancakes from the salvaged remains. A friend texts: "when life gives you lemons, make zucchini bread."

. . .

QUILTING IS ABSOLUTELY NECESSARY FOR ME NOW — THE PULLING TOGETHER, THE GATHERING OF SCRAPS WORN IN THE LIVING, THE DAILY LIVING, REMNANTS, EPHEMERA OF A LIFE LIVED IN DISPERATE PARTS. THE PULLING TOGETHER IN A WAY THAT BECOMES, CREATES ME. IN A WAY THAT MAKES SOMETHING ELSE. I NEED THIS PROCESS. I MAY DIE WITHOUT. PATCHWORK IS THE ONLY THING REAL TO ME AT THIS POINT.

2014, VANCOUVER: Working our booth at the first Vancouver Art Book Fair, having just finished giving our presentation, hot cup of complimentary coffee in hand, I scroll through the news on my tablet and click on a headline that reads: "What a Shaman Sees in a Mental Hospital." I click, perhaps because of Grandma, or because I watched too much She-Ra as a kid, or because I was raised among rural hippies who taught reverence for indigenous thought. Perhaps I click because I've grown suspicious of being called "too sensitive" by those who are not hippies, or because the stories I've loved most are not shelved under the category of Realism. Because Ana Castillo and Mário de Andrade resonate more than Jonathan Franzen. Perhaps I click because I do not trust Western medicine, its history or treatment of female pain. Or perhaps I just need to consider a different story. Whatever the reason, I click. The journalist explains that what West African shaman and author Malidoma Patrice Somé sees when he enters an American mental hospital are not people who are sick with Schizophrenia, Bi-Polar Disorder, Major Depression, but people open enough to be embodied by the spirits of ancestors in need of healing. In West African medicine, he explains, ancestor spirits need to be appeased, and those not at peace will come into another body in order to lay their past to rest. Such people in Africa, he says, would not be considered sick; they would be considered touched by the spirit world and, as such, be placed under the tutelage of a healer. They would be seen as budding healers themselves. He thinks what we call an epidemic of mental illness in the West is just the clamoring of our unburied past. He says it will keep touching the most sensitive among us until we all listen.

My muscles ice when I read this. A burning, a recognition, a hope. A holistic spin on the disorder that has derailed my living. His story slips into the cracks in my skin, and I hold it there a while. I consider Great-Grandma Mickey, the upholstery from her sofa that I found embedded in the flesh above my breast. Removing the orange and yellow flowers or their dark walnut background was not possible, for the patch had become part of my skin. I consider the recent epigenetics research linking trauma in humans to depression in their children and grandchildren. I consider my healing so far, the possibility that mine is not a broken story but a healing one.

I feel silly for wanting to trust this. I feel silly not because it doesn't sound real, but because my distrust of optimistic, New Age cannibalism is strong. Or perhaps because I've come to distrust everything. This distrust, my doctors say, is just one of the effects of this thing we call Depression.

[SEPTEMBER 2014, CALIFORNIA]

I peer into the shadows, join them for poisoned tea in the cemetery and find not malice nor wickedness, but pain. Just pain. My own and that of others. What we call Depression is an auto-immune disorder. My fragility is what saves me. I am told more women who suffer Depression are saved by their comfort with vulnerability than men. Men, as a result, are more likely to die by suicide.

My body becomes home to an older, graver weight. My face ages quickly, within weeks, and for months stays this way. A heaviness fills the skin, its symmetry distorted, contoured, shifting. As I heal, however temporarily, my face regains shape. It becomes me.

-

[UNDATED 2015, SACRAMENTO]

It is now 2:19pm, and I still cannot justify stitching on the quilt as legitimate studio work. I procrastinate, do chores, watch a movie, but don't just sit down to quilt. I fantasize about it, but cannot allow myself the permission today—there is so much *more important* work to do.

-

[8 JAN 2016, KIMMEL HARDING NELSON CENTER FOR THE ARTS, NEBRASKA]

"Well, women are used to worrying over trifles."

In Susan Glaspell's 1916 one-act play, *Trifles*, domestic spaces are overlooked by men in their pursuit of hard evidence to solve a murder while it is the women who uncover the subtle motives in the suspect's trifles—quilt blocks, a sewing box, an uneven stitch, a busted kitchen door. The male characters, who spend the entire play conducting their investigation in rooms beyond the hearth—that traditional domain of women—remain blind to the interior workings, to the complex rituals of domesticity that convey the wife's motives.

I stitched yesterday in the studio, transcribing oral histories with thread and, all the while, felt I was misusing the *important* studio space gifted to me here, the presence of the male painter next door looming as *legitimate* while my embroidery and quilting still felt inferior as a *decorative* art. It has been one hundred years since Glaspell's play was first performed, and decades of quilt scholarship have worked to elevate the craft to art, and I still feel the inferiority implicit in these mediums, in these *trifles* as I labor at them. How long does it take for intellectualizing and appreciation to scrub clean the layers that calcify under an "ism"?

–

In the 1980s, feminist theory inspired a group of MDs to investigate the correlations between women's experiences of depression in their own words, the cultural narratives surrounding depression, and the incidents and severity of the illness. The study was groundbreaking in its insistence on studying depression in women by cataloging and analyzing the experience of depression as told by the women who lived it. The study's authors found that American women told themselves stories anchored in male-centered values, such as strength by solitary action. They denigrated and downplayed their adeptness at things associated with femininity, like collaboration and interaction. The study concluded that these narrative tendencies were a major component in the women's depression.

What is most striking is that this clinical work, archived in a book I picked up second hand, seems to have made very little impact on our understanding of this disease. Yet the obviousness of the premise now seems so striking, thirty years later: listen to what women are saying, *in their own words*. Consider that as valid evidence. Consider that important. Thirty years later, and numbers in the publishing world, news headlines, court cases, all show us not much has changed; what women have to say is not read as important.

Someone said to me years ago that "you can gauge the health of a culture by the health of its women." As I write this, I hold one book in the galley stage with a major academic publisher and numerous prestigious awards to flash as permission to speak. As I write this, I am still convinced no one will listen. This is not just my own negative tracking or an individual case of writer's block and inner demons. There is statistical data now to back up my claims (because what a woman says needs to be validated by statistical data), alongside the echoing voice of the famous male writer: *no one wants to hear what white women have to say.*

But I say it anyway. I have decades of practice. I have piles and piles of diaries I've never tried to publish. I swallowed the lies like everyone else, let them hatch beneath my skin, but I crawled my way to the page and wrote with their bloodied pus when necessary. Like the women studied in the 1980s, I understand myself as broken. But it is not I who am broken. I live in a world shattered on all sides in a body that absorbs its pain, abstracts it, seeds it. My lymph nodes are simply swollen.

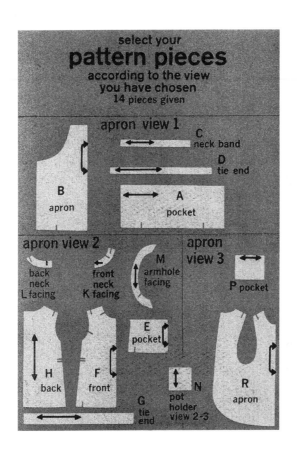

select your

pattern pieces

according to the view
you have chosen
14 pieces given

apron view 1

C neck band

D tie end

B apron

A pocket

apron view 2

back neck L facing

front neck K facing

M armhole facing

apron view 3

P pocket

H back

F front

E pocket

G tie end

N pot holder view 2-3

R apron

Everywhere I carry my North American body—South and Central America, Europe, Japan as reconstructed inside the Sacramento home of my World War II-surviving great-aunt—there is a physical layer I must shed in order to be in that place. In the case of my great-aunt's home, the shedding begins with the removal of shoes in the entryway—the unstrapping of the "heavy American boots" she says remind her of soldiers—and is complete within a few moments of her speaking directly to me. No small talk, no hiding, only this ability to see and to hold the threadbare places another human reveals. I am made acutely aware of a covering I carry in the place I most often call home, a shield crafted against the daily violence of life (t)here. It is a different kind of shield than the one I carry in Rio, where the violence is honest—armed robberies, murders, looting. There are other kinds of violence, too, of course: class warfare, hate crimes, rape. And yet my body remains open in particular ways as I walk the street, aware of very real danger. I am guarded, yes. I am hyper-vigilant all the time. Watchful. Weary. It is exhausting. The artist Alma Leiva crystallizes this feeling in her installation-photograph series *Celdas* (Prison Cells), in which she recreates the interiors of homes in San Pedro Sula, the second largest city in Honduras and a narco-city now infamous for being the most violent in the world. Leiva brings outside elements such as playground sand and teeter-totters inside, giving the intimacy of home space the weight of the prison cell it becomes in a city where danger outside seeps into everything. In her essay, "The Other Side of

Fear: Alma Leiva's Prison Cells," Dr. Tatiana Reinoza writes, "Home spaces are records of embodied and situated knowledge that allow viewers to connect the private with the collective sphere of experience." Reinoza goes on to cite the work of Amalia Mesa-Bains, María Brito and several artists in diaspora whose work focuses on intimate space as sites of violence and memory. These troubled intimacies are more common than we care to admit.

We drink excessively in Rio. Drinking allows dance and laughter, but the weight of history and its consequences are left unaccounted for, untended. The body doesn't close, but it craves numbing, a safety. We spend our days off indoors, attempting to unravel. When I am designing Leiva's exhibition catalog, years later, the sight of her photographs causes blood to rush to the surface of my skin. The feeling that radiates from the pixels haunts, finally distilled.

In the United States, it is the body that closes. It shuts in on itself to ward off the myriad micro-assaults to the senses: separation, subdivision, strip malls, the aggressive insistence of a thing called *personal space*, the sound of English in the way we speak it, the threat of white male terrorism that knows no consequence: mass murder, serial rape, shootings by police. My skin braces for the chill of contact: the handshake, the monotone speech that inquires about what I do for a living, the askance looks at any slip into vulnerability, desire, feeling. There is little space to be human here unless I am alone. And while solitude can be cause for elation, the prolonged isolation of one human from others causes the heart to stop. It incites death by a slow, steady calcification layered upon the flesh. This subtle closing is not the same as one that threatens immediate survival, but it threatens survival all the same. The body only breaks more slowly.

And what happens when intimate space itself is a warzone? Where does the body break then?

In empire, violence becomes a proud part of family narrative. *We are sons and daughters and grandchildren of heroes who fight in wars to protect our freedom.* We absorb the trauma of the soldier. As women, we are taught to absorb the trauma of the man, whatever man. We treat their pain as elevated, as honorable and just. And yet our domestic homicide toll accounts for more of our own deaths than all the wars we've been involved in since the Revolutionary one, but we do not honor these sacrifices or their repercussions. Violence becomes a comfort when tied to home life in this way, like the scent of vanilla or a wood stove.

Joy Harjo describes pressures on Native women during the early days of the American Indian Movement—the pressure to *take the hits for the cause*, to stand behind the men who fought and absorb their blows—in silence—at home. Alice Walker, Gloria Anzaldúa, Toni Morrison, The Latina Feminist Group, and the countless women I have interviewed articulate such paradigms as rampant throughout movements for civil rights. At one point, Gloria Steinem was blamed for the failure of ethnonational liberation efforts. Female liberation was seen—and is still seen—as counter-revolutionary, selfish, threatening to the larger good. Our stories of sacrifice are all-inclusive.

–

[5 JANUARY 2016, NEBRASKA CITY]

"Every public park in the state of Nebraska, no matter its size, displays a tank leftover from World War II."

2015, SACRAMENTO: A voice comes over the radio. Two voices. An interview. One says to the other something about the United States being a "post-alcoholic society," and that this has to do with the traumas of migration and genocide. I don't catch the names of either person speaking. I am off to some place important, some meeting. But all day my thoughts are weaving, lapping up one against the other, cracking open, burrowing into the next: Toni Morrison's *Beloved*; Rachel Yehuda's research on the children of Nazi concentration camp survivors; the scholar studying cycles of alcoholism in Irish immigrants, concluding that the hold of what is deemed a disease loosens by the fifth generation (its very own century of solitude); the feel of a street in the center of Rio; R and I running out of a forest in Michigan when a history we knew nothing about invaded what was supposed to be a picnic; the artist Stan Padilla speaking of the Post-Traumatic Stress Disorder that impacts the Miwok, Nisenan, and Wintu students he teaches.

We look to places like Sweden and Norway for their successful social infrastructures and overall cultural health, but fail to acknowledge the distinction in our histories, think it is a matter of mimicking certain social programs or economic allocations. But the body politic is still a body, and body is the thing that might just terrify us most here in the United States, its accumulation of history. It is a thing we value little and can barely stand to be inside. Even our language

separates us from it. We do everything conceivable to *liberate* our-
selves from it, to *escape* what we consider its confines, to *overcome* its
needs. Mind over matter. And so on. Perhaps it is a pain the body
houses that scares us. Perhaps it is our own collective hurting. Per-
haps the real work has something to do with learning to hold the
body, to brave the ache of being fully inside. This is to say nothing of
what is required were we to hold, even to just acknowledge, the pain
in one another.

Tonight I told myself a story of my life that echoed the story of my grandmother. And it's not even true. Some days I still have trouble untying one story from the other.

Our veins pump five quarts of blood in a full circle throughout our body every sixty seconds. If we breathe deeply, yogis say, we can purify this fluid. I am drawn to this idea that healing is possible by breath. And I wonder, if we do not breathe deeply, is it a matter of allowing the blood to cleanse itself in as many circles as it takes? Am I, at some level, just a body for this blood to pass through, to use to purify itself and then discard? Am I separate from my blood like my mother tongue assumes? Or is it like what Stephen Hawking says in *The Grand Design*, that, "in some cases, individual objects don't even have an independent existence, but rather exist only as part of an ensemble of many." Neurologists will tell us that, no, we are the bundles of connectors and fire alight in our heads, that the brain rules us, the mind is wise. Stephen Hawking, I am certain, would have other things to say about this and would likely suggest I avoid neurology as a source of metaphor. But I wonder what our science would tell us were its history not so heavily shaded by misogyny and racism. Would we have found intelligence, too, in the blood that clots and pounds out my labias? Would we have found it in our veins and marrow? In breast tissue or the gut? Would we make such rigid distinctions between fact and metaphor?

Something went wrong with legal paperwork for our civil union. I shut down now when this occurs, beyond my limits already.

Yesterday: 3x4 fotos com fundo branco, photocopies made of all legal documents, passport notarization. Bought myself a notebook, a beer, and a bolinho de bacalhão, made syllabus notes.

This weekend: Open bookstore for a party in the Fábrica. Evento na Comuna e feira com A Bolha Móvel. So much work. Want to do nothing today. Not an option. So fucking hot here. 134°F.

The U.S. coming undone. More police brutality toward Black men, children, women. Brazilians ask why. I find no adequate way to speak to this, except to speak of history and all that lies in our brutal forgetting and separation.

I think of the saying: *Americans never remember; Mexicans never forget.*

I think of Leslie Marmon Silko's *Almanac of the Dead* in which the narrator asserts that, without the restraints set in place by their families and home cultures, powerful European men in the Americas went mad, became sociopaths who raped, tortured and pillaged without consequence or remorse.

I think of how her book was banned in Arizona in 2010.

I think of Tia Blassingame's artist book elegies to the Black women, men and children slain in our streets. I think of her cotton scarves printed with lists of historical slave sites in New England, how she travels to forgotten spaces, to the quiet archives and parking lots and drudges up the misaligned bones, honors them with proper burial in elegant type and handmade paper, public ceremony under glass.

I think of Claudia Bernardi's luminous paintings made of ground bone and pigments, how she uncovers mass graves throughout the Americas with her forensic-anthropologist sister and holds the bones of the anonymous until her own body hollows and howls.

I think of the memory present in so-called marginal literatures and how memory runs counter to empire.

I draft a proposal for a course entitled, *Other Ways of Reading: Histories of Print, Narrative and Silence.*

2015, SACRAMENTO: At a reading, the old man who stopped me at a reading years back to talk about a book idea stopped me again to talk about the same book idea. Then he mentioned my performance he saw last fall. He said he didn't know quite how to describe it, but that the room had *filled with magic*. He repeated this several times. Then he went on to tell me that the women in his family were strong, were Huichol, and that he has carried their teachings throughout his life. He told me they inspired his career in architecture, but that he never felt safe enough in the US to admit this openly. But that now, at ninety, he *doesn't give a shit*. Now, he says, he tells everyone.

I have been encouraged by artists of prior generations to write the story of Billimae as I would have liked to see it unfold, to empower her character to change her story, to create a new one. This is how that story would read: woman escapes violence, finds brief, solitary peace, then another (better) man to redeem her and pardon all men. Or the variation: woman escapes violence, finds lasting solitary peace, perhaps among female friends.

But I do not write either of these stories. Writing over her story would betray all the brokenness I have known. I see too many women without hope feeling ashamed of their halting, of their bodies that have broken under the weight of pillage and sorrow. It would be sinister of me to project a happy ending onto Billie, onto other women. Onto my own torn places. Our culture is obsessed with forcing stories of individual redemption because we cannot see the webbing that connects our suffering one to the other. I can only expose the stitching.

[2015, RIO DE JANEIRO]

Saara. Sol de 14:00h cut off thought, ability. Recouro. Voices over
the loudspeaker: *tres por vinte! synthetic shorts!* água *gelada dois reis!
bijuteria barata!* A flying cockroach on a light bulb. Buying a string
of lights for the new bookstore. Rua Senhor dos Passos. Até Rua da
Conceição and beyond. Não rolou esfija hoje.

Taberna da Glória. Bus stop full. Woman applying something to
a man's face. Fake castle with plastic nativity scene on the median
strip. Farmâcia. Bus 434 to Garagau. Cactus in a planter. 21:03h and
sweat beads down my neck.

-

[JUNE 2015, SACRAMENTO]

Piecing. Piecing. The quilt a canvas today, hung on the bookshelf.
Appliquéing fabrics, materials, remnants as on a collage. Composing
this quilt like I compose a poem.

-

When I was younger, I imagined goodbye as a muscle in the body
that would strengthen with every use. Now I find it is a joint that
weakens, breaks down over time from too much wear, like the shoul-
ders of my father after decades of wheeling himself in a chair.

[6 JAN 2016, NEBRASKA CITY, NEBRASKA]

Halfway through a finishing stitch, this thought:

A strange new sexuality in me now, a kind of expanding sieve between my hips—an opening out, a deep giving. A heat extends to the birthing of children who are not biologically mine, but whom my body aches to feed. As if my desire for the messy, wet mingling of mature bodies is in some way in service of the beings growing around me. The feeling does not translate into a desire to make flesh from my own. Instead, I fall into a field of fully-grown bodies whose shared loving weaves a protective web for our collective offspring. A kind of invisibly woven armor formed when bodies—any consenting bodies—share their abundance one with the other. It is as if this sharing keeps the world in balance, keeps our future bodies healthy and safe from fracture.

Something about the plains in winter makes this *feel* clear. It enters me by way of the base organs: liver, ovaries, spleen.

2012, NEVADA COUNTY, CALIFORNIA: Her feet have swollen to twice their size, purple. I prepare warm water, olive oil, salt, scrub stone, nail clippers, cuticle clippers, soft bristled brush, that tool that pushes cuticles back from the nail. I remove her slippers, which are three sizes too small. She continues to walk on her swollen feet, ignores the pain. Her refusal to continue physical therapy has resulted in an inability to trim her own toenails, to bend at all. She becomes immobilized in a body for which she has seldom cared. She has cared for every body but her own. She has passed along this tendency by example. My sister and I spend our adult years unlearning this lesson. We spend our adult years unlearning many things.

I set her feet in the water basin, let them soak. I pull one foot from the water, set it on a towel, scrub the calluses, trim back the nails, slide the soft bristled brush across cuticles. She sips her tea. I return her foot to the massaging bath she's owned since 1980. This is the first time she's used it for herself, she says. She tells me stories I've heard many times already. I ask if I can record them to get the words right. She goes silent a spell. I take the other foot out, place it on the towel. She shifts in the recliner, sips her tea, asks me if I can check the fire. I stoke it, add a log. I sit back down on the green shag carpet, ask again. She eyes me, no smile: *I don't want your grandfather to hear us.* I pick up the stone and scrub dead flesh from her heal.

"... as if such a thing is learned, and remembered by the body, even if unspoken in words. It is as if the stories of the mothers are written into the child's beginnings."
—Linda Hogan

2014: Clean altar, light candle. Call to my great-grandmother, to her mothers.

There is a pain deeper than ancestors, a pain required by wildness and homing. Heavy. I touch hand to breast where her upholstery has been embedded. Tears absorb the bleeding. I hum a song of protection. I remove my hands. Both tingle. I open my palms toward the fire and her song rises. I circle the air with palms out, causing ripples. They still tingle, full of something. I dance her power away, agree to offer myself to this healing, but not at the cost of my body. I will not be taken down by this.

-

[FEBRUARY 2015, CALIFORNIA]

Songs come into my body as I stitch my nephew's quilt. They pound their way up from abdomen, spill out my lips before I notice what has happened, before I can silence myself if there is someone nearby. The impulse to silence is not mine, but it functions before I can stop it. I have to stitch another space for song to reemerge.

backing

Touch has a memory. O say, love, say,
What can I do to kill it and be free?
—John Keats

Give it life, not just detritus.

Call back, don't go back.

–

North America's colorful, post-World War I quilts were made of fabrics dyed using German recipes acquired in the terms of surrender. I wonder if this moment in our human story, in this United States story at least, perhaps in this post-colonial story of which the United States is part, is again a time of healing. I wonder if we, collectively, are not at a place in which we can begin to acknowledge the pile of bones strewn hastily at our backs. If we can inventory, again, the contents of our mass graves – the genocides and slaveries and silencing, the traumas and their ghosts – and begin to give ceremony to our dead behind us, as Audre Lorde called them. To perform burials, incinerations so that we might continue on in this living. I wonder if this is just a part of all living that we have forgotten. Because we are still dying. We still bury our dead in mass graves. We still murder ourselves. *In lak'ech. Tú eres mi otro yo. You are my other self.* A man dies at the hands of police. A woman dies at the hands of a husband. A family dies crossing the desert. Children are slaughtered inside a school. Our churches are still burning. There are many ways to kill a human. Each body a shrine to the violence left inside us.

That is the ideal, no?: that we do the work and do not numb ourselves. I battle a desire to numb in the face of this haunting, of the always coming fight. Some days the pain is too heavy. I binge on bad TV and boxed comfort food, smoke cigarettes, drink cans of beer. But even my own numbness allows me empathy with others who give into hiding. And this empathy seems vital somehow. Being able to hold our weakest parts means we can hold the weakest in others. And the most we can do for another human in this world is hold.

I spent decades studying the political and consciousness-raising movements of the 1960s and '70s as a child reared by hillbillies among back-to-the-land hippies in California, and later as an archivist and oral historian at one of the country's oldest Chicano-Indigenous cultural centers. I was privy to evidence of a particular kind of urgency that took place in that era, an idealism that needed to be wildly sure of itself in order to create a particular kind of change. Globally, major social shifts took place, affecting us all. Civil rights revolutions, counter-cultural rebellions, wars, resurging feminisms, decolonization, paradigm shifts, and solidarity. By the 1980s, a new breed of psychologists inspired by these movements' calls for cultural recovery, as well as by the research of Joseph Campbell and the methodologies of Jung, called for collective healing through the use of ancient stories and rites as medicine. Writers like Gloria Anzaldúa, Alice Walker, Toni Morrison, and countless others pulled silenced histories up out of unmarked graves to create new artistic and theoretical frameworks in and out of the academies. Hippies across the Americas and Europe looked to Celtic and other indigenous cosmologies as foundations for a new future. Sun Ra and his conspirators looked back to Africa and then to space. Hollywood turned to Norse mythology with She-Ra and He-Man in the cartoon medium. As early as the 1970s, groups like the Royal Chicano

Air Force responded by adapting ancient Mesoamerican ceremonies to contemporary life as a way to heal the ravages of history. In the case of urban Sacramento, the RCAF held Fiesta de Maíz, Fiesta de Colores, Fiesta de Jaguares, Día de los Muertos, Fiesta de Tonantzín. They brought in elders from across Aztlán and México, appointed elders inside their own communities, claimed the ancient rights as their own and adapted them to their present in neo-indigenist traditions of continuity that challenged Western cults of rupture and tearing.

In 2015, the National Institute of Mental Health estimated that 16.1 million adults in the United States had experienced major depression in the past year. The Institute defines depression as "a common but serious mood disorder" which "causes severe symptoms that affect how you feel, think, and handle daily activities, such as sleeping, eating, or working."

In 2011, the former President of Mexico told the BBC that "he holds the United States responsible for the violence in his country," which by then had resulted in 45,000 deaths as the state waged war on cartels. He pointed to the United States' high demand for illegal drugs as the underlying culprit.

In 2016, the Centers for Disease Control and Prevention reported that "drug overdose deaths and opioid-involved deaths continue to increase in the United States . . . 91 Americans die every day from an opioid overdose." We can blame the pharmaceutical industrial complex, the 24-hour news cycle, economic recessions, feminism, high divorce rates, lack of social cohesion and rites of passage, and a number of other potential causes. Some contemporary scientists seem to have dusted off Freud's theory of "primary masochism" from 1915 and renamed it the "selfish gene." The logic is that "your genes don't care if you survive to reproduce, as long as they do, and they exist in more people than just you. So they might lead you, their host organism, to sacrifice yourself if it sufficiently benefits your family members, who share many of your genes. Hence, people seek to maximize not only their own fitness but, inclusively, that of their kin too." We may also consider that The Human Genome Project has proved that the human genome, the collective term for genes, is not limited to our immediate kin, but extends to the whole of humanity. And if we consider that opiate-related deaths and suicide now disproportionately plague young white adults and that social privilege is paid for by those who do not enjoy it, we may entertain the notion that this epidemic speaks to a shared human desire for the health of the whole, a desire to lessen the burden for one's human kin by doing away with oneself. And while such lines of thinking may tangle through the body of the person who is depressed, this particular argument breaks down when we acknowledge that healing our individual and collective pain requires connection and not more cutting. It breaks down when we try to see this pain as part of its own healing.

In a young culture that insists upon unimpeded growth, it may be that we have simply ignored the imperatives of decay and stagnation as precursors to maturation and change. To borrow a question from the character Lucas in that 90s film classic, *Empire Records*: "What is with today, today?" At the risk of projecting, I would answer: grey. We are grey. That blurry grey of doubt and possibility and faded clothing and post-Post-Modern Xerox mash-ups. Copies of copies of copies. Meta everything. The grey of distancing from the original. The grey of the little rain cloud that follows Eeyore around, of the mental illness that pervades our historical moment and causes worry, judgment, spikes in pharmaceutical sales. But perhaps this grey is the grey of a necessary mess that occurs when *I* bleeds into *you* bleeds into *we* bleeds into *how*. Irigaray's *disruptive excess* now the faded backside of a patchwork heirloom about to become batting. Perhaps grey is right where we need to be. Perhaps grey is more akin to what psychologists like Paul Andrews and J. Anderson Thomson call the evolutionary purpose of depression. As Matthew Hutson reports in *Nautilus*, Andrews found that the symptoms of depression "appeared to form an organized system. There is anhedonia, the lack of pleasure or interest in most activities. There's an increase in rumination, the obsessing over the source of one's pain. There's an increase in certain types of analytical ability. And there's an uptick in REM sleep, a time when the brain consolidates memories. Andrews sees these symptoms as a nonrandom assortment betraying evolutionary design." The function of this design, he asserts, is "to pull us away from the normal pursuits of life and focus us on understanding or solving the one underlying problem that triggered the depressive episode." Maybe, then, the major problem is not the depression itself. Maybe the stories we inherit about the imperative toward growth and never stillness, never rumination, make the experience of this "evolutionary impulse" that much more desperate and isolating. Andrews and scientist Paul Watson continue on to argue that, rather than prescribe drugs, "it may be best to let depression work its miserable yet potentially adaptive magic on the social network under protective supervision." Like Carl Jung, Julia Kristeva, and the poets before and after them, this scientist proposes that what we call Depression may be a necessary descent into one or more of Dante's seven underworlds or the Aztecs' nine. In our current historical moment, what is the failure we need to inspect? Ours is a nation not yet comfortable with honest introspection. We love blaming the *other* and we have created plenty of them. And while this socio-economic depression may be where we need to be and where we are, where does the road out start? Where does it lead? Does that matter yet?

After thousands of years of human and cultural genocides, epochs of post-agricultural poverty, a century of global wars, we are left to the mending. We can colonize the moon, but that is only the repetition of an outworn, unsustainable model. That is nothing new. Perhaps all that is left is to sit down in front of the fire and grab a needle, sterilize it in the flame. Own up to ourselves, to each other. Start threading our body back together, one suture at a time, finding a way through the fragments.

This is where quilting becomes necessary, the pulling together of scraps worn in living, of soiled, used up, outworn shards, of all their ugliness and imperfection to create something that warms, protects, comforts—something else entirely, not something entirely new. That crazy quilts are an organic U.S. art form speaks to our continued tearing, wearing threadbare, assemblage, and appliqué. There are innumerable contemporary, community-based artists and collectives who choose not to break from their multiple and seemingly contradictory lineages, who continue to integrate story-as-medicine and body-as-site-of-knowledge practices into our present: Adaku Utah's Soular Bliss collective, the White Bison Wellbriety Recovery Circles, the Salmon Runs of the Pacific Northwest, the Círculo de Hombres, networks of Womb Priestesses, The Icarus Project, and many, many others. There is movement on the streets again on a massive scale, and the rhetoric of collectivism is again part of our global dialogue, even if its practice never ceased in places.

I want to believe something is shifting. I need to believe this to survive. I need the movement of a needle toward mending, away from imperatives of purposelessness and back toward them. In most cases in this culture, we no longer sew our own coverings out of necessity. Cheaper threads are available from foreign factories in box stores. There is no purpose, really, if we chose not to see the conditions of those very factories, in repurposing something like the quilt as form, except perhaps if we see our own continuity as having purpose *and* having none.

We come into this world through the bodies of other humans, their blood ours. As of yet, there is no way to escape this vulnerability. These bodies require that we move into our pain, birth ourselves through its tangle of blood and seepage. Too often we insist only on birthing forward our pain into other humans to escape the tearing open of our own hearts.

In the hills we protect those kinfolk who gouge the deepest holes. We defend them because we know their pain as our own. Some call this compassion, but it is not always compassion. Not all forgiveness works this way.

Contemporary psychologists after Rachel Yehuda document case after case of children of holocaust survivors, war veterans, refugees, and domestic abuse survivors who have never heard the stories of their parent's or grandparent's trauma, who have been shielded from it, even its acknowledgement, who have gone on to live lives that in some way strive to correct the past or heal it. Others may continue coping with their parents' grief through addiction and violence. I refused to believe blood is thick. I grew up on New Age ideals of *detachment* and formed deep bonds regardless of relation across geographies. My family and my home culture were things from which to break. They were toxic, diseased. But today I cannot help but wonder, given all the research, given my own body and its inclinations, if there is not something powerful in this fluid that pushes us to heal or at least manage some pain that is not entirely our own.

I unzip the nightmare. I lay it down in the gutter off a dirt road in Paraty. I lay it down in holes poked in linen, stitch after stitch. I lay it down, the weight of it, move it out of me—if there can be such a thing. We are composed of flesh and language that come from the flesh and language of others. There is no syntax native to humans.

It is a stitch, a repeated stitch, a dance, a song, a picking, a de-shelling of nuts, the processing of a deer, the chopping of cabbage, of chiles, a sifting through the beans, a hanging of the laundry, scrubbing the floors and washing the dishes only to wash them again. The hands at work wring out the blood. I haul up bones from the river and sit, listen to the screaming left in them. I hold up each bone to the light, wipe it clean of debris, realign it back into its skeletal form. I burn each bone to heavy ash to make an ink that can write, draw new stories. Only then will I put down my pen and sing off-key.

–

[JULY 2014, SACRAMENTO]

It does not matter the quality of my song, only the act of my singing.

But it does not end there. Things do not end so cleanly. Seams unravel in the wash, leaving loose strings we must burn or sever by biting. We may need to sew the same seam again, again, reinforce it.

For the last decade or so, it had been popular to be ambivalent. It had been the height of contemporaneity to not know anything for certain, to expose the process, to complicate thought and arrive at a precipice that promises to move us forward in becoming, but does not conclude anything except that maybe this is the moving forward: this complicating. As much as I share these convictions about the importance of questioning easy conclusions and the inherited ways we see the world, I cannot help but crave answers, desire cures and full stops at the ends of sentences. I have been taught to expect such things from life, or at least to impose such these things upon it. But perhaps there is something we have forgotten, something we left behind with the broken dishes in exchange for our post-Dust Bowl, recession-denying self-help, and at-the-height-of-empire optimism. Perhaps that something is simple, unadorned continuity.

My great-aunt, born on Hokaido Island, has been writing a novel for over twenty-five years. This novel takes place in wartime Japan. This novel's main character is a young woman. This novel is not finished. Sometimes it is not the finishing that matters.

When my Russian-born German grandfather died, he left behind a single diary written after he had returned from World War II, in which he had fought in the Allied Invasion of Normandy. In his diary, each day was dated in careful penmanship and read: "Shocked corn." That was all it said each day, every day, for weeks. One may wonder why anyone would ever bother to keep such an account, but perhaps it is just as honest a diary as any. Maybe documenting his movements in the same human way each day, tending to the most basic work as a means of bringing about the next day was enough. Nothing new or shiny or exciting about it. Perhaps, after all we call progress and all we call perfection, there is still corn to shock.

[13 JUNE 2015, SACRAMENTO]

I wake up late (6:50am), read for a few hours. I make coffee, toast a slice of bread, scrub the sink with borax, shoo away ants, re-hang the quilt, write in my slip, alternate between pushing back and suturing a heartache.

- - - - - - - - - -

Whip stitch down. Attach back fabric, turn edges in. Self bind.

— — — — — —

— — — — — —

— — — — — —

— — — — — —

— — — — — —

— — — — — —

glossary of terms

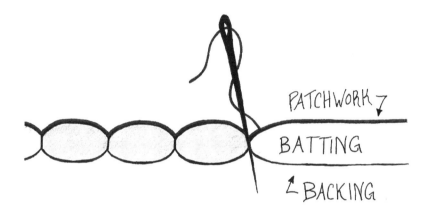

PATCHWORK

BATTING

BACKING

image list

Figure 1. *Language*. Cotton, thread. Stephanie Sauer, 2013.

Figure 2. *Untitled (BigBi)*. Napkin, ink. Stephanie Sauer, 2012.

Figure 3. *Excerpt I (from American Mountain People)*. Digital scan. National Geographic Society, 1973.

Figure 4. *Library Card Citation*. Found ephemera. Stephanie Sauer, 2014.

Figure 5. *Domestic Arts*. Rubber, cotton, denim, thread. Stephanie Sauer, 2013.

Figure 6. *Untitled (embroidery quote)*. Found ephemera.

Figure 7. *Embroidered Histories (came home)*. Cotton, thread. Stephanie Sauer, 2013.

Figure 8. *Untitled (emergency shelters)*. Paper, ink. Stephanie Sauer, 2008.

Figure 9. *Untitled (4-H Stamp)*. Found ephemera.

Figure 10. *Embroidered Histories (sugar in my gas tank)*. Cotton, thread. Stephanie Sauer, 2014.

Figure 11. *Ghost Sonar*. Paper, ink. Stephanie Sauer, 2011.

Figure 12. *Embroidered Histories (washer hose)*. Cotton, thread. Stephanie Sauer, 2014.

Figure 13. *Untitled (4-H Hat)*. Wool, metal. Stephanie Sauer, 1996.

Figure 14. *Untitled (4-H Sewing Class Instructions)*. Found ephemera. 1992.

Figure 15. *Untitled (Definition: patch)*. Digital scan. Stephanie Sauer, 2017.

Figure 16. *Untitled (Definition: patchwork)*. Digital scan. Stephanie Sauer, 2017.

Figure 17. *Untitled (Definition: patch test)*. Digital scan. Stephanie Sauer, 2017.

Figure 18. *Work Shirts*. Digital photograph. Stephanie Sauer, 2012.

Figure 19. *Untitled (Nevada County Map)*. Courtesy of the County of Nevada. Fred M. Miller and Pierce-Bosquit Abstract & Title Co., 1913.

Figure 20. *Excerpt II (from American Mountain People)*. Digital scan. National Geographic Society, 1973.

Figure 21. *Library Card Citation*. Found ephemera. Stephanie Sauer, 2014.

Figure 22. *Gold Dust*. Photograph. Stephanie Sauer, 2005.

Figure 23. *Embroidered Histories (he called my boss)*. Cotton, thread. Stephanie Sauer, 2015.

Figure 24. *Untitled (Love you Love you)*. Paper, ink. Billimae Alice, 2010.

Figure 25. *Embroidered Histories (with my daughter)*. Cloth diaper, thread. Stephanie Sauer, 2016.

Figure 26. *Excerpt III (from American Mountain People)*. Digital scan. National Geographic Society, 1973.

Figure 27. *Library Card Citation*. Found ephemera. Stephanie Sauer, 2014.

Figure 28. *Untitled (Herança exhibition documentation, ArtRio)*. Digital photograph. Stephanie Sauer, 2013.

Figure 29. *The [Almost] Ballad of Billimae Alice I*. Paper, Ink. Stephanie Sauer, 2013.

Figure 51. *Quilting is necessary.* Diary entry. Stephanie Sauer, 2014.
Figure 52. *Untitled (Pattern Pieces).* Found ephemera. 2014.
Figure 53. *Glossary of Terms.* Paper, ink. Stephanie Sauer, 2019.

works consulted

BOOKS

Bourgeois, Louise. *Destruction of the Father, Reconstruction of the Father.*

Bunkers, Suzanne L., and Cynthia A. Huff., Eds. *Inscribing the Daily: Critical Essays on Women's Diaries.*

Callahan, Nancy. *The Freedom Quilting Bee: Folk Art and the Civil Rights Movement in Alabama.*

Capone, Francesca. *Language is Image, Paper, Code, & Cloth.*

Cooper, Patricia, and Norma Bradley Buferd. *The Quilters: Women and Domestic Art, An Oral History.*

Crowley Jack, Dana. *Silencing the Self: Women and Depression.*

Diaz, Ella Maria. *Flying Under the Radar with the Royal Chicano Air Force: Mapping a Chicano/a History.*

Fry, Gladys-Marie. *Stitched from the Soul: Slave Quilts from the Ante-Bellum South.*

Herman, Judith. *Trauma and Recovery: The Aftermath of Violence—from Domestic Abuse to Political Power.*

Hidalgo, Luciana. *Arthur Bispo do Rosário: O Senhor do Labirinto.*

Hurston, Zora Neale. *Their Eyes Were Watching God.*

Ickis, Marguerite. *The Standard Book of Quilt Making and Collecting*.

Jamison, Leslie. *The Empathy Exams*.

Kapsalis, Terri, and Gina Litherland. *The Hysterical Alphabet*.

Lazaro, Wilson. *Arthur Bispo do Rosário*.

Lorde, Audre. *Our Dead Behind Us*.

Porter, Liz, and Marianne Fons. *American Country Scrap Quilts*.

May, Marian. *Decorative Stitchery*.

McCormick Gordon, Maggi. *American Folk Art Quilts*.

Montano, Judith. *The Crazy Quilt Handbook*.

National Geographic Society. *American Mountain People*.

Nelson, Maggie. *The Argonauts*.

Nin, Anaïs. *The Diary of Anaïs Nin*. Vol. 1-7.

Solnit, Rebecca. *Men Explain Things to Me*.

Tobin, Jacqueline L., and Raymond G. Dobard. *Hidden in Plain View: A Secret Story of Quilts and the Underground Railroad*.

Welsch, Robert L. *A Treasury of Nebraska Pioneer Folklore*.

Wheatcroft Granick, Eve. *The Amish Quilt*.

Winterson, Jeanette. *Why Be Happy When You Could Be Normal?*

Zambreno, Kate. *Heroines*.

EXHIBITION CATALOGS

Brandon, Reiko Mochinaga, and Barbara B. Stephan. *Textile Art of Okinawa*.

Centro Nacional de Folclore e Cultura Popular Iphan / Ministério da Cultura. *No "Vão" do Urucuia: Fios que Entrelaçam Saberes*.

Centro Nacional de Folclore e Cultura Popular Iphan / Ministério da Cultura. *Rendas nas Terras de Canaan*.

Morris, Walter F. Jr. *A Millennium of Weaving in Chiapas*.

Reinoza, Tatiana, and Luis Vargas-Santiago. *Counter-Archives to the Narco-City.*

University Gallery, Fine Arts Center, University of Massachusetts Amhurst. *Sheila Pepe: Mind the Gap.*

acknowledgments

Many thanks to Deanna Benjamin and *Drunken Boat*, *So to Speak*, Lisa Roni and *Aquifer: The Florida Review Online*, Terry Jordan and Nicole Haldoupis at *Grain Magazine* for first publishing excerpts from this book. Big thanks also to the Barbara Deming Memorial Fund for Women and the Kimmel Harding Nelson Center for the Arts for their early support of *Almonds Are Members of the Peach Family* as both publication and fiber art installation.

I am forever grateful to Carmen Giménez Smith, Sarah Gzemski, Emily Kiernan, Emily Alexander, Suzi F. Garcia, Steve Halle, and everyone at Noemi Press for their careful attention to this work and their ongoing dedication to independent publishing.

My deepest thanks go to all my mothers: Billiemae, Margo, Janet, Rosemary, Tatsue, Gladys, Isabel, Ana, Katherine, and Vera. Deep thanks also go to my uncle, for the stories and wood stacking lessons; to my father, for giving me life, twice; Janell Lacayo for trespassing right alongside me; Ella Maria Diaz for the vital talks and also vital cigarette breaks; Shannon Zeller for the singing and the hitchhiking; Kate Gartrell for the sewing circles; Joel Araújo por a fé e o apoio; Caleb Dardick and Carolyn Murphy for the ongoing support, long dinners, and lazy river days; Alice Randall for helping me to seed this work; Megan Douglas for the naming and the sharing; Kelly Morse for the warm words on the cold plains; Dale, Yon, and Janelle for the healing; and to Frank and Art for offering Luna's Poetry Unplugged as one of the best places to take artistic risks.

E a Rachel Gontijo Araujo, por tudo (e também por o atelier mágico onde este projeto nasceu).